The Bizarchives
Weird Tales of Monsters, Magic, and Machines

Presented by
The Midgard Institute
of Science Fiction & Fantasy Literature

THE HORROR BENEATH

C.P. WEBSTER

THE BIZARCHIVES

Copyright © 2023 by C.P. Webster and The Bizarchives

All rights reserved.

No part of this book may be reproduced in any form or by any electronic or mechanical means, including information storage and retrieval systems, without written permission from the author, except for the use of brief quotations in a book review.

CONTENTS

1. The Viewing, October 1977 — 1
2. March 1978 — 18
3. Antrobus — 55
4. the Recce — 95
5. The Solstice — 141
   Epilogue — 177

CHAPTER ONE
THE VIEWING, OCTOBER 1977

"*Vielleicht...*" Konstantin von Hallerstein said, pushing the papers back across the cluttered desk. "That is, *perhaps* Mr. Wingood... perhaps," the German added noncommittally.

Clive Wingood winced inwardly. Von Hallerstein's stern, heavily accented voice, really did get under his skin.

"Perhaps?" the estate agent echoed, feigning surprise but still irritated by von Hallerstein's now familiar aloof disdain. "But Marchley Howe is a real opportunity Herr von Hallerstein! It's in a prime location with a splendid pedigree; historic properties like this one aren't often on the market *and* it meets all your very exacting specifications! Of course, it will require some... modernisation. But what an investment opportunity!"

Von Hallerstein shrugged, seemingly unimpressed.

"And that's why I said *perhaps*."

The tall German stood up and pulled his dark overcoat on quickly.

"I've got business to attend to. I'll view this house tomorrow morning at 11... If that's convenient of course?"

From his tone it was apparent that von Hallerstein did not care less whether it was convenient or not. Wingood rubbed his hands together as he too rose to his feet from behind his desk.

"Yes Mr. er, *Herr* von Hallerstein, that will be quite alright, I do have another appointment, but I can reschedule that. Erm, if..."

But von Hallerstein had swept out before the estate agent could finish his sentence.

Sighing, Wingood sat down heavily. He smoothed his thinning hair back onto his head and pressed the office intercom.

"Debbie, could you come in for a moment please. And bring me a fresh cup of tea, would you? I need it."

Wealthy clients like von Hallerstein were, of course, very welcome, but this one really had been most troublesome to work with, even for a man of Wingood's wide experience. Von Hallerstein was brusque and demanding and had provided a strict list of requirements that brooked no deviation. For a wealthy bachelor he seemed particularly pernickety. Amongst other stipulations, there could be no near neighbours, at least four acres preferably with some woodland and of course it had to be a property of distinction. But Clive Wingood was a man up to the challenge. The office portfolio of 'Wingood and Harper' contained some of the most exclusive properties in the county and his sales were up. When clients wanted a country property, he was the man to find it. Whenever he was close to a sale, he felt a boyish excitement. But if this sale happened it would be even better. If von Hallerstein signed, as Wingood hoped, then the estate agent was going to celebrate properly.

Marchley Howe had been quietly on their books for years, a cumbrance that Wingood's recently deceased partner, George Harper, had (very surprisingly) bought at auction on an impulse and for a song. The house had been in the same family since the eighteenth century, but the house itself was much older, built on the site of an old priory, it was an ancestral home that seemed to have grown out of the sandstone of the landscape itself. When the elderly and reclusive spinster who owned it had died just shy of her ninetieth year, it seemed that her only heir was a distant cousin who lived in Liverpool. The cousin had not even bothered to cross the Mersey to attend the funeral let alone view the house, but their instruction to the local solicitor representing them had been clear - conclude a sale as quickly as possible. Mortley's, a large Liverpool firm of property brokers, had been given the job of disposing of the ancient pile (much to both Harper and Wingood's chagrin). Yet, despite a buoyant market and an enormous amount of interest, enthusiasm quickly waned when the house was inevitably viewed. Once they had arrived for a viewing, nobody seemed to *want* Marchley Howe. Nobody that is, except Wingood's business partner, the late George Harper. When finally, nearing desperation, the vendor had put the house up for auction with only the meanest of reserves, Harper had bid compulsively. Shortly after the gavel fell, he had dazedly phoned the office and tried to explain to Wingood that the property was too good an opportunity to miss. But as he had paid the auctioneer's assistant the deposit monies, Harper's perplexed and staring eyes had revealed that his decision was as much a mystery to himself as it was to his astounded partner Wingood. For a time, it had soured their professional relationship, and the old pile sat festering in their property portfolio for years despite all of their best efforts to shift it. Harper spent as much of the business's money as he dared in order to keep the house in a marketable state, but much of the upkeep came ultimately out of Harper's own pockets. In the end, Marchley Howe had been, in Wingood's decided opinion, the very cause of Mr. Harpers' untimely demise.

The idea of offering it to von Hallerstein had come to Wingood in the middle of the night, one of those rare moments when the unconscious reaches out with clarity to the conscious mind. Wingood had been sleeping unusually badly, he was at his wits end after a series of disastrous viewings that had led to von Hallerstein as good as declaring that Wingood was incompetent. But his night-time anxiety had quickly evaporated when Wingood remembered Marchley Howe.

Why hadn't he thought of it before? It was strange. After all, he had mused, it ticked off all of von Hallerstein's requirements. The longer he had considered it, the more Wingood began to believe that he could just be on the verge of finally offloading this burden of a property onto someone else. His instincts were seldom wrong. If he was cunning, the profit on this one would feather Wingood's nest nicely, very nicely indeed.

A smartly dressed young woman, entered the room holding a cup and saucer of steaming tea. She looked at Wingood questioningly.

"Another pleasant chat with our dashing German friend?"

Wingood groaned theatrically as he took the proffered tea. He drank deeply then sat back and sighed.

"Marchley Howe, Debbie," he said.

The secretary paused at the office door turning quickly in disbelief.

"Marchley Howe?!" she repeated, surprised despite her usually unflappable nature.

Wingood's smug smile confirmed it.

"Well, I never," she tutted, "but no good will come of it, it never has."

Wingood shook his head.

"That house has been like a great albatross the weight of a white elephant around my neck" he insisted.

"You're mixing your metaphors," Debbie chided him smiling.

Glancing at her and grimacing, Wingood continued.

"He *will* take it, I'm certain he will. It's just the sort of place for a pretentious character like that. Once he has signed then..." he shrugged expansively. "Once he has signed, well then, Marchley Howe is *his* problem."

. . .

The next morning dawned bright and fair. After eating a substantial breakfast, Wingood pecked his wife Doris on the cheek, and left the house. He was in a buoyant mood when he pulled his silver Jaguar XJ6 out if his driveway and for once the morning suburban traffic was light. Quite soon, he was speeding south along an 'A' road towards his meeting with von Hallerstein. None of the disastrous previous viewings disturbed Wingood this morning, he felt confident once more. As he finally steered his Jaguar off the busy 'A' road and reduced his speed to a sedate twenty miles an hour, his mood was further lightened by the sudden quiet and leafy smell of the autumnal country lanes that he was now meandering through. Best of all, the sun was shining brightly, and the sky was clear, great sales weather! He glanced at his watch. Plenty of time, Marchley Howe was only another five or ten minutes away.

In his mind he went over his strategy for the viewing. Grounds first? he wondered. He knew that the garden services should have been out recently so the parkland in front of the house ought to be looking glorious. But Wingood quickly rejected that idea out of hand. No, no, he concluded, von Hallerstein must first be led up the front steps of the house and enter through the ancient doors into the oak-panelled entrance hall. That should make von Hallerstein feel as if he were the squire himself. That would create a striking first impression. The panelled walls of the entrance hall were topped by carved wooden shields painted in a variety of bright heraldic designs. Yes, that should resonate with an aristocratic snob like von Hallerstein. Wingood allowed himself a smile.

After another ten minutes, Wingood slowed the car and then turned into a narrow, tree-lined road marked 'private'. Beyond the wooden 'private' sign the entrance to the lane was guarded by two large square gateposts built of wide blocks of moss-covered red sandstone. Wingood glanced at the name 'Marchley Howe' carved into the front-facing stone of the left-hand pillar as he climbed from the car to unpadlock the gates. Once they were open, he got back into the car then accelerated down the lane.

The steep-sided track first traversed a deep broadleaf wood now a riot of autumn colour. There were ten acres of it Wingood reminded himself. Finally, he saw bright sunlight ahead and emerging from the dark cover of the trees, Wingood could see Marchley Howe itself. Despite his irritation with Harper's legacy, Wingood had to admit that it was an impressive sight.

The ground floor was built of large blocks of weathered sandstone, presumably much of which had been part of the old priory. The patterned red tiles of the roof provided a stark but beautiful contrast to the black and white half-timbering of the upper floors. It was a property so typical of the older houses of the county. Whatever else the former owners had done, one thing was certain, they had, by design or through ignorance, preserved an historical gem. It still puzzled Wingood why this property had been so hard to sell. But today would be different, he felt it!

The road now led straight towards the house across tree-studded parkland. Wingood was relieved to see the grass had been freshly mown and everything did indeed look splendid. He drove the Jag up to the front of the house and turned the engine off. A deep silence fell as the sound of the engine died. Wingood climbed out of the car and patted his jacket pocket. He felt the reassuring weight of a large iron key. He glanced at his watch, ten-thirty. Wingood strode quickly up the three, wide stone steps that led to the high front door. The formidably thick and heavy dark timbers of the door were reinforced by black iron studs. Wingood retrieved the key from his pocket and put it into the ornate iron lock, there was a heavy click and Wingood pushed the right-hand side open. He sniffed and frowned; the place needed airing but that was no surprise.

Wingood quickly proceeded to open the windows on the ground floor, moving from oak panelled room to room and, with a practiced eye, quietly assured himself that everything looked in good order. Once he had returned to the entrance hall, he paused and looked about the space. This was the first impression of the interior von Hallerstein would receive. Wingood smiled once more, it really did look splendid. Shafts of bright sunlight were now shining through the three stained-glass windows above the entrance. The windows themselves were relics of the original priory, rescued from the ruins and reinstated in the fabric of the house when it was built on the priory's foundations. The red tiled floor sported a myriad of pretty colours from the light above. Then Wingood shivered with supressed excitement. This was it!

He paused, had he heard a motor?

Closing the door behind him, Wingood stepped out of the cool interior back into the warmth of the sun. Yes, von Hallerstein was coming, there was his car now. The estate agent waited for his client to arrive.

Von Hallerstein's black Mercedes purred to a halt behind Wingood's Jaguar. Wingood waited but von Hallerstein sat still behind the steering wheel. Wingood raised his hand in welcome and smiled. Still, von Hallerstein remained seated inside his car.

'What the devil is he up to?' Wingood thought trying not to show his irritation.

He walked tentatively over to the driver's side door of the Mercedes and tapped on the glass of the window.

"Good morning Herr von Hallerstein, fine day, isn't it?"

Von Hallerstein looked at him wearily from inside the car then reaching for the handle, opened the door and got out. He stretched and sniffed.

"Good morning Mr. Wingood" he said not looking at the estate agent. Instead, he looked up at the house appraisingly and ran his hand through his thick, iron-grey hair. "Shall we begin?"

Wingood nodded, suddenly feeling uncharacteristically flustered.

"Yes of course, follow me please."

He paused by the entrance and, attempting to regain his composure, he cleared his throat.

"This is of course the main entrance to the house; it is believed to be the original timberwork from the Tudor..."

Von Hallerstein reached forward and opening the door, quickly stepped past Wingood and entered the house.

He stopped in the centre of the entrance hall and looked carefully about him. Then Wingood saw that the German had closed his eyes and seemed to be smelling the air. Wingood watched puzzled then realised von Hallerstein had asked him a question.

"I'm sorry I was miles away... what was that?"

Von Hallerstein sighed impatiently.

"I said how many acres of land about the property?"

"Ah... yes, ten acres of deciduous woodland, the woods you drove through on the way here, and a further twenty-four acres of pasture and parkland," he stammered, almost robotically, he knew he needed to get a grip. "In addition, there is a further five acres of conifer plantation on the northern edge of the property. The house is situated in the very heart of the land, yet, despite its splendidly private position, you are still within quick reach of all the major arteries, rail and airport..."

Von Hallerstein suddenly raised his arm for silence then reached across and rested his hand on the elaborately carved newel post at the base of the stairs. He closed his eyes again.

"Hmmm."

Wingood hesitated.

"Herr von Hallerstein? Shall we look at the rest of the

ground floor? Through here is the great hall, a very fine living space with a rather unique original fireplace..."

Von Hallerstein opened his eyes and turned to look at Wingood as if suddenly remembering that he was there.

"A cellar? It does have a cellar?"

Wingood blinked. He could feel himself blushing like a teenager as his composure continued to evaporate.

"A cellar?" he muttered dully.

"A *cellar*," von Hallerstein repeated. "Well, Mr. Wingood?"

Wingood nodded and pointed to a stone-arched door beneath the rising staircase.

"Here Herr von Hallerstein," he said walking across the hall. "I'm afraid the electricity is off at the moment, so you won't be able to see anything down there... Or shall I fetch my torch from the car?"

Von Hallerstein strode across to the cellar door and pulled it open. He closed his eyes once more and inhaled as the cool and musty air rose out of the dark aperture beyond.

"Yes Mr. Wingood, do fetch your torch there's a good fellow."

Mumbling an apology, Wingood turned and retraced his steps to the front door.

"I... I'll just be a moment..." he stammered as he walked outside.

Wingood took a deep breath. 'Come on Clive get a grip,' he thought. 'After all, he's never asked to see the cellar first before, perhaps it's a good sign?'

Wingood opened the boot of the Jag and rummaged

around for his torch as he pushed aside a pair of green wellington boots and a blue anorak. Finding the large rubberised black torch, he quickly checked that it was working before closing the boot and returning to the house.

"Herr von Hallerstein?"

Von Hallerstein was nowhere to be seen.

"Er... hello?" he called up the stairs.

"Down here."

Starting, Wingood turned and walked over to the cellar door.

"Herr von Hallerstein?"

Wingood fumbled with the torch and turning it on, shone the beam down the worn stone steps. The light fell on von Hallerstein's broad back, now halfway down the stairs.

"Do come on Mr. Wingood," the German urged testily.

Wingood nodded.

"Ah, yes, sorry."

He walked falteringly down the ancient stone steps shining the torch before him.

As they reached the base of the stairway Wingood shone the light around in order to reveal the space around them.

"It's a good-sized space and you can see that it is dry... the ambient temperature is I believe perfect for wine and the humidity is about right too."

Von Hallerstein raised his hand impatiently.

"Listen," he said.

Wingood looked about him.

"I'm sorry Herr von Hallerstein what am I listening for?"

"Did you feel that draught?" the German asked.

Wingood remained mute, unsure now what to say.

But von Hallerstein shook his head.

"Never mind... Tell me, how far does this space extend?"

Feeling that he was back on safer ground Wingood replied:

"The cellar dates from the Old Priory itself as the house was built on its more than adequate foundations. In fact, these cellars are the original undercroft of the priory, a multi-roomed space, but all perfectly sound as attested in the engineer's report from 1975. One can see that the rather lovely pillars belong to an older ecclesiastical period and..."

Von Hallerstein snorted.

"I don't want a potted history Mr. Wingood, how big is it, how far back does it lead? How deep does it go?"

But Wingood only shook his head foolishly.

"I... Er... it's a large space and..."

Von Hallerstein put his hand out impatiently.

"Give me the torch, would you? And then wait for me upstairs."

Dumbly Wingood passed the torch to von Hallerstein who promptly turned away and began to walk into the darkness, following the beam of the light before him.

"Ah, Mr. von Hallerstein, I'll just be at the top of the stairs then..."

Left in the sudden darkness, Wingood shivered involuntarily then, with his arms stretched out in front of him, slowly began to shuffle towards the dim light at the base of the cellar stairs. When he finally reached the top of the steps and stepped back out of the cellar door, he sighed and quickly mopped his forehead with his handkerchief. He had always hated the dark. Damn von Hallerstein and his stuck-up manner, why did he get under his skin so?

Wingood walked over to the front door and peered outside. Sunshine and birdsong. Wingood inhaled deeply, his former enthusiasm for the sale now ebbing, he just wanted to leave.

Wingood was still standing there looking across the landscape when he heard the echoing tread of von Hallerstein's shoes as the tall German climbed back up the cellar stair.

"This is the one, at last."

It was the first time Wingood had ever seen von Hallerstein smiling though his face was oddly pale, and he seemed unaccountably out of breath.

"Very good Mr. Wingood, I'll take it," the German said bluntly, taking a deep breath.

Wingood smiled stupidly and blinked.

"Eh?"

Von Hallerstein stared at him impassively.

Wingood swallowed.

"Ah... well that's wonderful news Herr von Hallerstein," he spluttered. "Would you like to see over the rest of the house now...?"

But shaking his head, von Hallerstein walked past him.

As he climbed back into his car the German paused as if in deep thought.

"I will come to your office first thing in the morning. In

order to discuss the details, you understand. Right now, I have much to prepare."

And with that he started the Mercedes' engine and drove off.

Wingood stood there for a moment in a daze. Then his smile returned, and it remained there for the entire drive back to the office.

Von Hallerstein was as good as his word.

The next morning at nine, just as Debbie finished unbolting the front door of the estate agency, von Hallerstein's black Mercedes pulled up at the curb outside.

"Our German is here," the secretary called cheerily in the direction of Wingood's office. "I'll make a pot of coffee."

Wingood straightened himself up in his chair and adjusted the papers before him. A moment later, he heard von Hallerstein talking with Debbie. There was a knock, and the secretary pushed the door open.

"Here is Mr. von Hallerstein for his appointment Mr. Wingood."

Wingood stood as the large man strode in. They shook hands and Wingood offered him a seat.

"Coffee Mr. von Hallerstein?" Debbie asked from the door.

"Yes, please," von Hallerstein answered without turning.

"Thank you, Deborah," Wingood said.

The two men now sat opposite to each other across Wingood's desk.

"Well Herr von Hallerstein," Wingood began smiling, "I hope you are still interested in Marchley Howe?"

Von Hallerstein frowned.

"I think I was quite clear yesterday Mr. Wingood. I *will* take the house."

Wingood smiled once more.

"Excellent Herr von Hallerstein, you won't regret it, it's certainly a unique and beautiful property. Who is representing you? You will need to give me your solicitor's details and I will make all the arrangements once we have completed our business here."

Von Hallerstein reached into the inside pocket of his overcoat and withdrew a large rolled manilla envelope.

"Everything you need is in there, my contact details, identification, etc., and of course the details of my solicitor."

Wingood nodded.

"Excellent, excellent."

"There will be no survey," von Hallerstein continued. "I am happy to proceed without it; my solicitor has been instructed to act with all haste to ensure that this business is expedited as quickly as possible."

"And here are the papers regarding the property and its land." Wingood picked up the small pile of papers that contained room dimensions, maps of the land and descriptions of the services, as well as a brief summary of the history of Marchley Howe.

As von Hallerstein took them, Wingood said:

"Also, as you can see, the asking price is listed at the top of the first page."

Von Hallerstein took the papers and glanced over them.

"I'm not here to haggle, Mr. Wingood," he said, a flicker of a smile now touching his lips. "I will pay the asking price. As I've said, I want this matter concluded as quickly as possible. As soon as I sign, and the house is mine, I will transfer the money to your preferred bank account. I trust you *will* contact my solicitor immediately?"

"Yes, Herr von Hallerstein," Wingood said smiling warmly, "it will be my pleasure."

Wingood reached across to the office intercom.

"Now, how about that coffee to seal the deal?"

CHAPTER TWO

MARCH 1978

The sale of Marchley Howe had been completed unusually quickly. There had certainly been no delays and, Wingood suspected, von Hallerstein's solicitor had been 'financially encouraged' to prioritise his client's business and accelerate the finalisation of the sale. Whatever the case, once the business had been completed, Wingood had not heard anything further from von Hallerstein.

Now this.

Wingood sat back in his armchair and read the headline of the Chronicle again.

West German TV Star Missing! Foul Play Suspected - Police Still Baffled.

Wingood poured over the article once more to double check. No, there was definitely no mention of the estate agency, that was one thing at least. Of course, he had already spoken to the police. A young plain clothes officer named Evans had come into the office a week ago to ask about the sale and anything else that Wingood knew about von Hallerstein, especially how his state of mind was. Wingood had been surprised to hear that von Hallerstein was in television. As he had explained, von Hallerstein's personal documents had simply stated that he was a writer and journalist. Certainly, as Wingood had been able to demonstrate with his files, there had been nothing irregular about the financial side of things. As for von Hallerstein's state of mind, Wingood had answered that he thought the German rather odd but that wasn't yet a crime, was it? The policeman wanted to know why Wingood had thought him odd. But all Wingood had managed to convey was that von Hallerstein had been rude and demanding. To this the policeman had merely raised an eyebrow. Wingood had answered the rest of the policeman's questions as honestly as he could, the policeman had taken the file promising to return it once it had been 'processed'. The file was dropped back into the office by a uniformed officer a couple of days later.

The Chronicle's article was continued on page three. There was a brief explanation that the 'striking looking' Konstantin von Hallerstein was a 'big' West German tv star as well as a best-selling author. It went on to disclose that 'the German millionaire' had recently moved to England in order to buy a mansion in the countryside and complete his latest book. According to the Chronicle, the police had gone to Marchley Howe on a routine check when von Hallerstein's West German tv production company had formally contacted the County Constabulary for help. As there was no working telephone line at the property, the police had sent two officers in a panda car to Marchley Howe to check on the new occupant of the manor. But they had found the front door unlocked and the house empty and deserted. However, various signs (the newspaper article had not elaborated what these were) had suggested to the police that foul play had occurred. Von Hallerstein's Dusseldorf-based agent had also become increasingly concerned that they had not heard from their 'star' for over a month after New Year. The agent was offering a £3,000 reward for any information leading to von Hallerstein's safe return.

Then the writer of the article had really gone to town. Aside from the more bizarre speculations about the possible involvement of organised crime and the KGB – after all, the newspaper had insinuated (rather tenuously Wingood thought), von Hallerstein had written a book about Mafia links to Soviet intelligence - the article had closed by citing 'historical sources' about witches, a curse and black magic all centred on the Marchley Howe estate.

Wingood threw the Chronicle aside. He did not consider himself a gullible man nor was he inclined to believe that old wives' tales and local legends were anything other than fanciful nonsense merely devised to thrill, warn or frighten the young and the overly credulous. He believed this to be equally the case (if not more so) when that modern purveyor of speculative chatter, the local 'rag', ran articles discussing 'curses'. Of course, Wingood knew full well that Marchley Howe was a house with a strange, even a bizarre, history. Long before the estate agency had come into possession of the property, the house was well known to have had a somewhat chequered past that included murder of some sort. But there were bound to be legends and at least one 'veiled lady' in any self-respecting country home. Yet, von Hallerstein's singular disappearance had unnerved Wingood more than he cared to admit, and, despite himself, the sensationalist tone of the newspaper article had had its own effect on him. Now, Wingood wanted to do a bit of further research on the more 'colourful' historical aspects of the house before he decided what to do next, if indeed there was anything to be done.

After supper, Wingood washed the dishes whilst his wife Doris, prepared herself upstairs for an evening at the Bingo. At length they left the house and the couple drove into the town centre. Wingood parked outside the Bingo Hall, and they agreed to meet back at the car at nine. After watching her go inside, he turned and walked leisurely down the high street in the direction of the town library. When he arrived, he was pleased to see that the lights of the building were still burning brightly. But the night air was chill and Wingood rubbed his gloved hands together as he quickly made his way through the revolving door into the library itself.

Inside the door he paused for a moment and inhaled the comforting smells of polish and books.

A young, long-haired librarian with a sparse blond beard, whispered across to him.

"We're closing in half an hour sir."

Wingood nodded.

"I won't be a minute," he answered reassuringly. "I know what I'm looking for."

He made his way over to the stack that contained books relating to local history. It was a sparse collection, but he saw just the sort of book that he wanted right away. Selecting it, he quickly flicked through the pages, looked at some of the photographic illustrations, and read the blurb on the back cover. Then, satisfied with his choice, he checked the book out and walked back outside. Wingood glanced at his watch and smiled. Plenty of time still for a pint and a sly cigarette in 'The Red Lion' before the Bingo was over. Book under his arm, he headed for the pub.

Later that evening, Wingood entered the dark bedroom and made his way slowly to his own side of the bed. Taking off his dressing gown and then kicking off his slippers, he pulled the covers back and carefully leaned his pillow against the headboard. Then he glanced somewhat furtively at Doris's back. She still seemed asleep, but he knew from long experience that she was a disturbingly light sleeper. Quietly, he reached down and switched the bedside lamp on and then, very slowly, he climbed into bed. Making himself comfortable, he lifted the library book and looked at the cover.

The cover image was a colour photograph of a silhouetted standing stone, crowned with a halo of long reaching rays of sunlight.

"What are you reading now Clive?"

Wingood jumped then rolled his eyes at the peevish tone of Doris's voice.

"Oh, are you still awake dear?" he said, looking guiltily at the book in his hand.

Trying now to placate his wife, he continued:

"The book's called 'Our Mysterious County: From Folk Tales to Flying Saucers' by someone called Jack Antrobus. It's about *our* county Doris, there's bound to be some interesting stuff in here."

But Doris seemed unimpressed.

"Flying saucers! You're cracked if you believe that sort of thing! I did know an *Antrobus* once though, what was her name again... Margaret! That was it, Margaret Antrobus. She had a goitre on her neck."

She turned now and fixed Wingood with a sharp look.

"You're always reading. Can't you turn the light out?"

"No Doris," he said now trying to sound firm. "It's work stuff, I need to gen up on a few facts."

Doris sighed and rolled back over onto her side.

"It's that ruddy house of George's, isn't it?"

"No dear, just go to sleep, I won't be long."

Wingood opened the book once more and tried to concentrate. He flipped to the Contents, there it was, 'Marchley Howe', page fifty-five. Wingood quickly thumbed the book to the relevant chapter and began to read.

The Devil and the Squire – A Tale of the Hellfire Club?

. . .

Marchley Howe is an old house with a long and, as we shall see, troubled history. Long before the building of the present manor [see the map, Figure 15], a twelfth century monastic priory had been founded on the site, set rather picturesquely in the hilly heart of the northern half of the county. The priory was not large, but county historians suggest that it was built in the Romanesque style and that it was richly endowed by its noble patrons. The founding monks had been from of an obscure Hospitaller order who, upon their return from the Holy Land in 1120 A.D., had successfully petitioned the Baron of Halten, one William fitz Nigel, for a large parcel of land in order for the establishment of a priory. Oddly, very little further information is known about the monks. A Mediaeval scholar and contemporary of the founders of the priory, was Robert of Deva. In his 'Liber de Spirituum', Robert makes a strange, footnoted reference to the order, describing that the monks themselves had been drawn to this specific site, by the widely held belief that an early British saint named Albin, had lived out his days there in a simple stone cell. St. Albin had, according to Robert of Deva (citing the Venerable Bede's 'Ecclesiastical History of the English People'), singlehandedly routed an armed 'heathen assemblage' with a rod of birch as his only weapon. Later he performed 'many other myracles' and is even reputed to have raised a dead man back to life [Author's Note: For more on this saintly 'resurrection' see my first book 'Ghosts and Ghoulies of our Country Lanes']. The monks who built their modest priory on this site, did not record any further miracles under their rule, indeed all records of the priory are scant throughout the intervening centuries, but it is assumed, that they did at least manage fairly well from the surrounding land. Certainly, there were still some monks there to be violently ejected when, during the Reformation, a rioting mob, made up of 'villeins' from the surrounding villages, descended one night on the priory and burnt it to the ground. The surviving monks were, according to extant Parish records, vigorously pursued across the countryside until 'none yet remayned'.

After passing into the hands of the Crown, the land was eventually purchased by one Hugh de Venables in 1545. De Venables was a minor noble with large ambitions, and he raised a fine house in the Tudor style using the foundations of the semi-demolished priory. Apart from a brief scuffle during the Civil War (when a small party of Roundheads had famously been chased across the Parish bounds by Squire Thomas Venables and several 'likely' village lads), Marchley Howe might have faded into the county annals as another ancestral pile with a shrinking estate, inhabited by an ever-degenerating aristocratic strain.

However, it was during the eighteenth century, when all records of the Venables line itself finally ended, that Marchley Howe became associated with infamy. Edmund Venables became the last squire at Marchley Howe to bear the Venables name when his father, John Venables, finally succumbed to the consumption in the terrible winter of 1739. The news of the old squire's death cannot have affected the hard-hearted debauchee more than the long-awaited chance of achieving his birth right and the confident conclusion of resolving certain pressing gambling debts. Once he had satisfied his creditors, Edmund Venables hastened to leave London and claim his inheritance. He was served on this journey by a short, ill-favoured creature named Jenkins who had claimed the title of his master's valet for several years. Jenkins carried under his cloak a brace of loaded pistols, but the riders were not molested on their long journey and the men arrived safely at Marchley Howe after five days travel.

The pair soon established themselves within the old walls of the manor, each according to their station. Jenkins prowled the servants' quarters like a malign spirit, springing out of the shadows to terrify a serving lad or grope at a young maid. All the servants, man and woman alike, called him 'the goat', and all shuddered at his burning black eyes and lecherous leers. Nor did the master waste any time in shocking the rural squirearchy with his own depravities. In the first year of his residence, the new squire had been involved in three drunken brawls. More seriously, there had been an allegation against the squire of a 'vile assaulte', that had left a young milkmaid 'with childe'. The charge had not stuck but the damage was done. The once proud name of Venables was now mired by scandal across the shire.

Seemingly unabashed by his loss of reputation, Venables had as much an evil temper at home as he did when he was abroad, and this, in combination with the unsettling presence of 'the goat', and the gossip about the squire, resulted in most of the Marchley Howe servants leaving Venables' service in short order. Soon, besides the sneering, uncouth Jenkins; only a pair of elderly retainers, a doddering, white-haired old man and his equally bent wife, remained to attend on the squire. Despite the new squire's oppressive tyranny, the elderly servants were too old and too loyal to the name of the 'old' squire to even consider seeking work elsewhere. Marchley Howe had been their home as well as their labour for many decades. As a result, they suffered Venables' mockery and cruelty for several years until, at last, death itself released them. The boorish squire, now only attended by the swarthy Jenkins, passed his days soused with claret, habitually ensconced by the Great Hall fire and snoring with his dogs. Only the need to shoot at something could occasionally rouse him to leave the house and mount a horse.

Then, in the year 1750, after almost eleven years of scandal and barely suppressed local outrage, a change occurred in Venables that coincided with the visit of one Sir Francis Dashwood. Dashwood was later infamous as the leader of the notorious Hellfire Club, and he was an old crony of Venables, with the two becoming very well acquainted as mutual patrons of the 'George and Vulture' inn during Venables' dissolute years in London. Nothing concrete is known of Dashwood's visit to Marchley Howe itself, but it seems apparent that from that time on, Venables was a changed man in his habits, withdrawn and quieter in his moods [Author's Note: For more on Dashwood and the shocking revelations about his other visits to our County, see my forthcoming book 'Hellfire at Harvest Time: Murder and Sex in the County Seat']. Venables' rural neighbours were at first glad of the surprising transformation. However, as it turned out, this change was not for the better.

In the spring of 1751, a seven-year-old child named Ann Moore, mysteriously vanished from the garden of her home where she had been watching over and playing with her three younger siblings. Her mother had only become aware of the misfortune when the wailing of her younger offspring roused her from her housework. The smaller children were inconsolable, and no meaningful explanation could be extracted from them about the disappearance of their sister save that a strange peddler had been seen talking to her over the garden gate, just before she vanished. A search was begun once the yeoman father returned from his work in the fields. The searchers roamed the surrounding landscape, combing streams and woods far into the night, carrying flaming torches to make their way through the dark. But by dawn the search had revealed no clue to the fate of the missing child nor any trace of the mysterious peddler. Tragically, Ann Moore was to be only the first of a series of strange disappearances of children over the next two years. Very soon a frantic hysteria began to contaminate the surrounding countryside...

Wingood's eyelids began to droop, it was time to sleep. Rubbing his eyes, he skipped two pages before resuming reading.

The affairs of the 'new' squire Venables would culminate in Venables and his servant's mysterious disappearance in the year 1753, only hours before a magistrate and a group of well-armed militia men forced an entry into the house itself. What was discovered in the dark cellars of the house are still open to conjecture...

Eyes closing, Wingood let the book drop from his hand. His snores began even before the book had settled on the floor.

Wingood had never been an imaginative man and he could not recall a time when he had ever been disturbed by dreams or especially nightmares. Sleep for Wingood was habitually an unconscious state of blissful restfulness through which he whiled away the hours of the night. But tonight, he did dream and when he woke in the morning, though he could remember little of the dream itself, he felt shaken and tired. As the sun rose and shone brightly into the couple's bedroom, it's warmth and light did little to shake off the lingering vague impression of cold dark dread.

That Saturday, Wingood sent Debbie home early and closed the office a half an hour earlier than usual. Things had been quiet and Wingood could not focus properly on work in any case. After bolting the front door and pulling the blinds down he returned to his office and sat down at his desk to think. He had read the chapter on Marchley Howe in Antrobus' book again, fully this time. It was disturbing reading, even if it was difficult to fathom for an unimaginative man like Wingood. However, whatever devilry Venables had really gotten up to, according to 'Our Mysterious County', everything had been well documented and could be verified. All of it, from the visit of Dashwood, the missing children, the suspicions in the neighbourhood right through to the magistrate's visit to Marchley Howe to arrest Venables, and Venables convenient disappearance, all apparently true. There were even several corroborating stories about 'paranormal' activities at the property right up until the 1950s. Wingood scratched his head. Whatever the history of the house, Wingood felt confident that von Hallerstein had not been carried off by vengeful spirits. No, von Hallerstein was too substantial a man for that. In any case, Wingood had sold dozens of country houses with supposed spooky histories. Most people were only too delighted to hear the stories, if anything, ghosts and a mysterious history were often a selling point. But *something* had happened to von Hallerstein and Wingood felt an uncomfortable feeling of responsibility. He knew his conscience would continue to itch if he did not make at least a token effort to find out more.

Then he had an idea.

He walked through to Debbie's desk in the reception area. Then he opened her filing cabinet and began to quickly look through the files. Closing the top drawer and muttering to himself, he opened the second drawer and began over. Then he stopped.

"Ah ha!"

He pulled the file out and laid it down on Debbie's very tidy desk. Opening it he flicked through a pile of neatly stapled correspondences until he found what he was looking for.

An invoice.

'Bob Latchwood, builder, electrician, carpenter – Kelsall 26783'

Wingood had recommended Latchwood to von Hallerstein during their last meeting. If von Hallerstein had hired him then perhaps the handyman might be able to shed a little further light on the matter. Wingood took a notepad from Debbie's desk and picking up a pencil, scribbled the number down and returned to his office.

He stared at the notepad for a few moments then picked up the telephone and dialled the number.

The phone rang for several seconds before a woman answered it.

"Hello 26783?"

Wingood cleared his throat.

"Hello, is Mr. Latchwood there please?"

There was a pause before the woman replied.

"He's not here at the moment, he's on a job. Who's speaking please?"

Wingood suddenly sensed from the coldness of her tone, that, for whatever reason, the woman was suspicious.

"Yes, of course," Wingood replied. "My name is Clive Wingood, Bob has had a fair bit of work from my estate agency," he explained candidly. "That's 'Wingood and Harper' in Netherton."

The woman gave a sigh, seemingly of relief.

"Oh good, Mr. Wingood is it. That's fine. Can I take your number? He can call you tonight when he's home."

"Certainly," Wingood answered somewhat bemused. "I just wanted to have a quick chat about work stuff, that's all. Please do ask him to phone me this evening."

He gave the woman his home number and rang off after thanking her.

Wingood stretched back and looked at his watch. He considered going for a round of golf, but he could see that it looked like rain outside. No, he would go home and see what Doris was up to. Sighing, he reached for his raincoat and hat.

. . .

When the phone eventually rang that evening Wingood had answered quickly. He had been distracted all afternoon and had, much to Doris' annoyance, been unable to relax, waiting for the expected call.

"Oh, hello Bob, thanks for ringing back."

"So, Mr. Wingood, got some work for me?" a gruff voice asked expectantly.

Wingood coughed lightly.

"Not exactly Bob, I just wanted to ask whether you were contracted to do some work on Marchley Howe."

The line went quiet for several seconds.

"Aye, what of it?" Latchwood finally replied guardedly.

Wingood thought for a moment.

"Bob, as you no doubt know the buyer of that property is... er... missing."

A grunt from the other end of the line.

"Aye, I 'eard, and I've already spoken to the police. What's this all about Mr. Wingood?"

Wingood sighed.

"Oh, I don't know. It's just odd... I'm trying to find out..."

But Wingood paused wondering what indeed he was hoping to find out.

Latchwood was quiet for a moment, then he said:

"Do you know the Mummer's Arms in Kelsall?"

"Yes, of course?" Wingood replied, surprised.

"Good, can you meet me there tomorrow at lunchtime? Say twelve thirty? You can ask what you like then."

. . .

Wingood drove over to the 'Mummer's Arms' at Sunday lunchtime as arranged and, after parking his car, walked inside the old inn.

He recognised Latchwood straight away, a large man wearing a black donkey jacket and jeans. The public bar was fairly busy. Latchwood spotted him and beckoned him over.

"Hello Bob," Wingood said as he signalled to the barmaid. "What are you drinking?"

Latchwood smiled.

"That's very kind of you Mr. Wingood, I'll have another pint of best bitter please."

He ordered their drinks and then Wingood followed Latchwood into the quieter environment of the inn's 'snug'. They sat down at a table next to the large fireplace that dominated the cosy room.

"Thanks again for agreeing to see me," Wingood began. "Can you just tell me what work you did and what it was like, anything that you remember might be useful."

Latchwood looked at him dubiously.

"You sound like a copper Mr. Wingood," he said taking a sip of his beer. "I've had bloody journalists phoning me as well... mind you, I wouldn't mind that three thousand quid..."

Wingood shook his head.

"Just tell me about the job. You were doing the rewiring for von Hallerstein?"

Latchwood nodded.

"Yeah, we did the wiring alright, in the cellar that is, but it was a big job."

Wingood blinked.

"Just the cellar? But the whole house needed rewiring?"

The handyman shrugged.

"Look mate, we were contracted to fit the electric lighting in the cellar only. Have you seen how big it is down there? There's arches and passages and a few other rooms. All churchy looking too, pillars and carvings and the like. Anyway, when we was done, he could light up that place like a football field. I suppose with his money he wasn't worried about the electric bill... He even got in a diesel generator in case of power cuts, a bloody big thing that was a nightmare to get down them stairs. It was a strange job but we was done before Christmas and he paid us cash and that was it."

Latchwood shook his head as he lit another cigarette, looking at Wingood almost furtively.

"It *was* creepy mind you; I don't mind admitting that."

"Creepy? In what way?" the estate agent asked.

The man frowned and supped deeply on his pint before continuing.

"Well, like Vernon for example, he's my apprentice. Now Vernon, he's a good lad, been with me for a year now, never gives me any lip or owt like that. Always does as he's told. You know, a good 'un. But he wouldn't work alone down there, not a bit of it. I was annoyed at first, it meant the job would be a lot slower, but I didn't have the heart to bollock him about it. After all I didn't like it too much down there myself."

Wingood sipped at his lager and lime.

"So, what did you do."

The handyman looked at him and narrowed his eyes.

"If you ever say owt about this to anyone I'll know it was you..."

Wingood blushed.

"I'm just trying to find out about what might have happened... later on," he protested. "As the estate agent I do have a... a vested interest in knowing you know."

Latchwood looked around them as a young couple entered the snug and passed their table, then, ensuring that they could not be overheard he continued.

"We kept together," he muttered, "me and Vernon, made sure we did everything in pairs like a couple of frightened schoolgirls." Latchwood was still looking about him warily. Then he lowered his voice even further. "But we 'eard, noises, like, thought we... saw things."

Wingood raised his eyebrows incredulously.

"Noises? Things?"

Latchwood looked at him then as if daring him to mock him. He pulled on his cigarette and exhaled a cloud of blue smoke before replying.

"Well, I'll just say this. We wouldn't stay after dark, that's all. We said nothing to *'im* of course, but I just made sure that each day we was packed up and ready to go as soon as the light began to fade. The kraut didn't say owt though, he seemed just as keen to shift it too when it grew late."

Wingood shook his head.

"I'm sorry what do you mean. Are you saying von Hallerstein didn't live in the house?"

Latchwood nodded darkly.

"Not as far as we knew, no. Not at least until we finished the electrics in the cellars. Until the day we finished the job, he was just as keen to be off at nightfall. Can't say about what he did after we was done like, but given what's 'appened..."

Clive Wingood removed his flat cap and ran his fingers through his thinning hair distractedly.

"What about furniture and decorators?"

Latchwood shrugged.

"I never saw anyone. It was just a big, old empty 'ouse. There was no furniture, nowt like that, except in the Great Hall. He had a gas camping stove in there, and a sort of fold up chair, there was a pile of books and a typewriter as well. But there wasn't no bed. And it wasn't my place to ask him now was it?"

Wingood frowned.

"I suppose not..."

He looked at his watch absently.

"You didn't say about these noises, the... the things you thought you saw?"

The handyman grinned slyly now and winked.

"Buy me another pint Mr. Wingood and perhaps a spot of brandy and I'll tell you alright."

Nodding, Wingood reached for his wallet and went back to the bar to order the drinks.

When he returned to the table Latchwood drained his

beer and reached across for the new pint and the glass of brandy.

"Very nice," he said as he quickly downed the brandy.

"Well Bob?" Wingood asked.

Latchwood reached into his pocket for another cigarette. "Well…" he began.

But nothing Latchwood told him helped clear anything up for Wingood. Indeed, after his chat with Latchwood, Wingood was more confused than ever. As for the noises and 'things' that Latchwood and his apprentice had thought they had heard and seen, well, to Wingood it sounded like they had been jumping at shadows. After all, he reasoned to himself, the eye can play tricks on you in the dark and the strange history of the house was well known in the area… No, Wingood decided, no, they had simply let their imaginations run away with them, not that he had said that to Latchwood's face of course. He had politely thanked the handyman for his time and had left the inn, driving home still puzzled. Wingood remained unusually quiet as he and Doris had eaten their Sunday roast. Doris seemed to enjoy the silence.

Business for 'Wingood and Harper' had been brisk for the rest of the month and Wingood had had little time to dwell on von Hallerstein's mysterious disappearance. Even the Chronicle seemed to lose interest as no further information had been forthcoming from the police. After one more rather lurid article, now relegated to page 5, a blatant example of what used to be called yellow journalism Wingood thought, the Chronicle quietly let the story drop.

And so, the strange disappearance of von Hallerstein might have eventually slipped out of Wingood's mind altogether.

Then he received the parcel.

It came during a busy day of viewings and telephone wrangling. Wingood had been in and out of the office all morning whilst simultaneously trying to resolve a particularly sticky problem caused by a young, overzealous surveyor. But five o'clock came around at last and Debbie locked and bolted the agency door. She entered Wingood's office to say goodnight. Wingood was just replacing the telephone receiver as she entered.

"That's it then Deborah, all done for today..."

He looked up then frowned noticing that Debbie was carrying a parcel in her hand.

"What have you got there?" he asked.

"Parcel for you, it's marked 'private'," she answered, "so I didn't open it." Then she smiled mischievously. "Are you expecting a present from a secret admirer?"

Wingood gave a short bark of laughter.

"If I were twenty years younger Debbie, I'd ask you to come and have a drink with me."

Debbie tittered and her cheeks reddened.

"You'd have to get through Mike first, he's outside in the van waiting to give me a lift home."

Wingood smiled. Then he saw the parcel again.

"Give it here then and get off with you to your beau."

THE HORROR BENEATH

Debbie placed the parcel on Wingood's desk.

"Have a nice evening Mr. Wingood, I'll see you in the morning."

Still smiling, Wingood watched her leave.

"Yes, goodnight Debbie..."

He heard the back door close after the secretary then he turned to study the parcel.

"What's this then?" he mused.

Wingood looked at the handwritten address on the front of the brown package.

Suddenly, a cold chill passed through him. He *knew* that handwriting. It was unquestionably von Hallerstein's script.

Wingood gasped and involuntarily pushed the parcel away. He stood slowly; his eyes fixed on the handwritten address. His name, his business address...

Turning away, he strode over to a large green filing cabinet and opened the top drawer. Reaching in, right to the back of the files, he drew out a half-jack of scotch. He broke the seal and unscrewed the cap, surprised by the shakiness of his hands. Then he took a deep pull of the whisky. He grimaced, then drank again. Carefully, he screwed the lid back on and replaced the bottle in the filing cabinet. Taking a deep breath, he turned around and retraced his steps back to his desk.

Reluctantly, he reached across for the parcel.

It was large and rectangular, neatly wrapped in brown paper and tied with string. The postage stamp was locally franked. Again, he looked at the writing on the front. There could be no doubt. Hands still trembling, he took his paper knife and nicked through the string. Then, he ripped the paper off to reveal a simple flat cardboard box. Not hesitating now, Wingood lifted the lid gingerly and looked inside.

There was a large, bulky manilla envelope. Wingood lifted this out and opened it. Inside were the deeds to Marchley Howe. The familiar iron key sat heavily at the bottom of the envelope. He put these aside on his desk and reached for the final object. A smaller white envelope with his name on the cover.

His hand shaking once more, Wingood tore the envelope open and pulled the folded letter out. Slowly, he began to read.

Sunday 18th December 1977

My Dear Mr. Wingood,

I appreciate that the receipt of this parcel must have come as something of a shock for you. For this I truly apologise. You must, by now, be well aware that something has happened to me. It was, therefore, always my intention that you should only receive this parcel if I had failed in my endeavours, and failure means, I am certain, no return. If you are reading this, then I have, alas, failed.

This parcel will have been posted to you from my hotel - it does not matter now that you should know which hotel or what name I have stayed under. On my last evening in the hotel, I will settle my accounts and ask the desk clerk to forward this parcel on my behalf should I not return to the hotel in three months' time at the latest. He will post it to you, he will be generously rewarded for his discretion.

As I look about me, I see only prosaic normality. It is a modest, but nevertheless pleasant, hotel room. Needless to say, I am comfortable enough. All of the lights are burning brightly, lighting the room brilliantly. That is good. The small dressing table contains a pyramid of spare lightbulbs, stacked neatly in their cardboard containers. The lights are always on now and I have kept it so, even in the daytime. Yes, everything is in its place... Yet, I feel something else. Something is feeling, groping...

But I am getting ahead of myself my dear Mr. Wingood. I am in an understandably disconcerted mood tonight. I have no doubt that you must now think me eccentric, mad even.

All I can ask is that you read this letter and believe me. <u>You must read it all</u>. Then do what you think best. With this letter I enclose the key and the deeds of the house, these I pass most reluctantly back to you. Reluctantly, because I am sorry to pass this burden back. You seemed a nice man, I think you English would say 'a good chap'? Even your name reveals your nature. Goodness counts for something. And through the agency of your good will, together we might yet contain this.

I have not lived in Marchley Howe since I purchased the house from you. It is not a place where one could comfortably spend time. The mask of loveliness that it cloaks itself in is quickly dissipated by the advent of twilight. How the old spinster managed to live there alone for all of those years is a mystery to me, but then not everyone is as sensitive to these things. My reading of the house's history suggests that the other, older 'resident', has remained dormant for a very long time. But its hour is approaching once more or else the indications are all wrong. No, I have not lived there, though I have spent all the daylight hours I dared to there.

I arranged to have constructed a whole lighting system to ensure maximum brightness for those hours when I conducted my work in that crypt. Light, is, a meagre protection. Last week, as I watched the workmen hurriedly leave for the last time, I knew that the thing I had come to do would soon begin in earnest. Nor could I waste any more time. The days are growing ever shorter, and the winter solstice is almost upon me. The solstice is, I am certain, the key. With the workmen gone I commenced the task of revealing the hidden depths of that now well-lit crypt. It was hard physical labour, aggravated by an almost overpowering sense of malice. Such malice! But I had to continue. I hammered and levered at the old worn slabs of stone in the floor like a man possessed. Finally, there was a sudden roaring collapse and an almost overwhelming cloud of foetid air and choking dust. I swooned then but as the dust cleared, I saw that I had indeed succeeded. Before me lay a dark maw, a wide circular pit, like some ancient well, at least twenty feet in diameter. I paused then and looked into that aperture with wonder, even for a moment forgetting both my fear and my aching limbs. The bright lights of the crypt revealed that the well was lined with huge and smooth, cyclopean blocks of stone that appeared to be some kind of fused granite, quite distinct from the local sandstone and intricately constructed in a style weirdly reminiscent of certain Andean ruins. The great oaken timbers that had been used to hold the heavy floor slabs that had sealed it must have been rotting away for years, centuries even. The beams had partially collapsed and tumbled downwards following my labours. I had at last revealed the entrance to the deeps. Yes, it was there, just as I had anticipated it would be.

Immediately I hastened to fetch a rope and, making it fast to one of the many carved pillars that support the vaulted roof, I made a first impetuous descent, lowering a bright halogen lamp by the longest electrical lead that I had and carrying a small electrical torch between my bared teeth. I shudder at the memory as I write this. I will not describe the lower place that lies at the base of that long shaft save to say that it was clearly very ancient and exceedingly cold. But I must return there on Wednesday night, down the deep well and along that winding passage that leads to the maddeningly alien and frigid chamber so far below. It is in that dismal subterranean place where my work must conclude. I am as prepared as any sane man might be.

What is this all about I imagine you are asking yourself? You may by now perhaps, have heard something about me in the press. Suffice to say I have built my career on somewhat salacious but always 'evidence-based' investigative journalism.

But that is only one part of who I am. It is not the whole.

For many years I have been an associate member of something I will call here 'The Company'. It is not the organisation's real name of course, but it will serve. I am sometimes approached by 'The Company' to investigate a specific case. Some of the particulars of the project are shared with me and, if I choose to take the case, then I am provided with all means necessary to assess the situation and act accordingly. As I said, I have had many years' experience and have had many successful resolutions.

The Company offers a discreet, professional service, attending to what might euphemistically be referred to as 'unusual' problems. Contracts from high political office around the world are not unknown. Marchley Howe was a little different though. In fact, it was an 'in-house' commission, the result of certain, curious recent discoveries by The Company's own research team. But on that I can say no more.

The particulars I received about the assignment were sparse but clear. I knew that Marchley Howe was purchased in 1972 by your own Mr. Harper. I also knew that the house remained, 'untenanted'. This was what I had expected given the legacy of the house's history. The way was clear, I would make the relevant enquiries with your agency and, as I hoped, you would eventually offer me a chance to look at the house itself. I now wonder if your initial reluctance to show me the place was significant. It was certainly very frustrating!

I am not at liberty to discuss the nature of the problem at the house. I will say only this, the problem is <u>beneath</u> the house. But on Wednesday night, I will go beyond my inadequate barrier of electric light, I will lower myself back down to that lowest chamber, dark and deep and dreadful.

My dear Mr. Wingood please mark these words.

<u>Do not return to Marchley Howe, ever</u>.

Fire would cleanse the house, but it would not reach deeply enough below to effect lasting change. Explosives might do it, but the risk of trying this is too great and the result would remain uncertain.

Therefore, I implore you with the utmost sincerity and hope of your compliance – <u>do nothing</u>. Others may come to complete the work should I fail tonight.

But I implore <u>you</u> once more. <u>Do not return to Marchley Howe</u>. Never again pass the gates of that long drive. Have nothing more to do with the house. Lock the key and the deeds in your safe and forget them. Let that place fade from mortal memory.

<u>Let it rot alone</u>.

Perhaps then, all will be well. Perhaps...

There the letter ended followed by von Hallerstein's elaborate signature.

Wingood sat down heavily and exhaled.

"He must have been bloody mad... As mad as a March hare!"

Looking once more at the now crumpled letter in his hand, Wingood decided to have another tot of whisky.

The next morning, Wingood phoned Debbie and informed her that he would be late getting to the office. Then, dutifully, he took the letter to the county police headquarters. After some time seated in the reception area near to the desk sergeant, he was at last invited into a nearby office by a grey haired, stern looking man in civilian clothes.

After closing the door behind them, the policeman shook Wingood's hand formally.

"I'm sorry to have kept you waiting Mr. Wingood."

His voice was polite, Wingood could detect a burr in the accent, Scottish perhaps.

"I'm detective-inspector MacDonald. I've been leading the investigation into Konstantin von Hallerstein's disappearance."

The policeman pulled a pair of spectacles out of his jacket pocket and put out his hand for the letter. Complying, Wingood passed the envelope over. MacDonald took the letter and carefully opened it whilst continuing to stare disconcertingly at Wingood.

Wingood shifted anxiously in his chair.

"Have you anymore news about what might have happened to him?" the estate agent asked nervously.

The policeman shook his head and continued to read.

"I'm afraid I can't discuss the particulars of an open case Mr. Wingood, you understand of course."

Wingood nodded.

"Of course," he managed.

There was a period of uncomfortable silence as MacDonald scanned the letter. Finally, he placed the letter on the desk.

"Aye, well, poor chap. We'll have this compared with a sample of his handwriting of course but it seems clear to me that he did lose his mind after all..."

Wingood coughed and glanced at his watch.

"I'm afraid I'll have to be going soon, I've got to get to the office…"

The inspector nodded and stood quickly.

"That's fine Mr. Wingood, you get yourself off to work. We'll keep hold of this for the time being."

MacDonald looked at the letter once more.

"There is one more thing…"

Wingood looked at the inspector expectantly.

"It says here that he included the deeds and the key? Where are they?"

Wingood was nonplussed.

"In the safe, at the office I mean. I can bring them, I never thought…"

The inspector's smile quickly returned.

"No, that's fine Mr. Wingood. I will send a constable over to collect them. I doubt they will shed any further light on things, but we would like to look at them anyway."

He smiled again then ushered the flummoxed estate agent quickly out of the office.

"Thank you Mr. Wingood. We'll be in touch should we need anything else, and of course should you receive anymore… 'parcels', then do let us know at once. Thank you."

As Wingood opened the door to leave, the inspector called out to him once more.

"Oh, Mr Wingood?"

Wingood looked back quizzically.

"Yes, detective-inspector?"

The policeman pursed his lips and stared at Wingood intently.

"Remember Mr. Wingood, we suspect that something 'untoward', happened to Mr. von Hallerstein at Marchley Howe..."

He looked at Wingood keenly.

"Marchley Howe is no longer a crime scene Mr. Wingood, but I would respectfully ask you not to visit the site. As for the deeds and ownership well, in these circumstances I wouldn't like to speculate, that's up to his beneficiaries if any exist." The policeman became suddenly stern. "Keep that key locked in your safe until I can send a constable to collect it. Thank you."

Wingood left the police station and completed his interrupted journey to the estate agency, still puzzled by the arrival of the strange parcel and the cryptic messages the letter contained. He told himself that von Hallerstein was simply a madman, a real bona fide nutter. It was in the hands of the professionals and that was that. Having passed this letter on, he decided that he would do just as von Hallerstein had instructed. He would do nothing about it at all.

After returning to the estate agency, he had quietly informed Debbie that a policeman might come by for the key and the deeds to Marchley Howe that were now back in his possession. Wingood did not elaborate any further and Debbie was puzzled by this and very much intrigued. But she held her peace and did not ask any further questions for now. As it turned out, a constable arrived to collect the deeds and key that very afternoon.

Following his interview with detective-inspector MacDonald, Wingood determined to put the matter out of his mind once and for all. The rest of the week passed by quickly enough and as April arrived, spring seemed finally ready to take the offensive. The days were now clearly growing longer and even noticeably warmer. With the advent of better weather, Wingood felt an allied renewal of enthusiasm for his work that coincided with a markedly buoyant spring housing market. Most of all, with each passing day, Wingood was able to push the matter of Marchley Howe further and further into the dimmest recesses of his conscious thought. He had matter-of-factly reassured himself that von Hallerstein's disappearance was simply one of those mysterious things that happen from time to time. Wingood reasoned that the police were better left to their investigations without his involvement. And besides, the letter that Wingood had received from von Hallerstein had clearly indicated that the German had written it in a most dubious state of mind.

There the matter might have ended for Wingood save for a chance meeting at the end of that very month. Once again, the unpleasant matter of von Hallerstein's disappearance was forcefully resurrected in Wingood's thoughts.

On a rainy Friday evening near the end of April, Wingood had driven up to Manchester to attend a masonic meeting at his 'mother lodge'. His jag had roared along the motorway, the melodious tones of Andy Williams, booming out of the speaker of his car's cassette player. Wingood had been looking forward to the evening for some time. As a past master and current treasurer of the lodge, Wingood was a regular participant in both ceremonial and social events. Sometimes he even took Doris along, she had really enjoyed the last Ladies Night. Although Wingood took his masonic duties very seriously, what he really enjoyed was the camaraderie. It was a chance to be alone with other men, to relax and to talk. Besides, the connections that Wingood had forged with other 'brother Masons', had also proven to be more than useful in his own professional life.

Once the order of ceremonies was complete for the evening, most of the freemasons gathered in the lodge's bar for a drink. Wingood joined them and ordered himself a large scotch and soda. He spent the rest of the evening chatting, laughing and exchanging stories with Martin Rudge, a fellow estate agent and an old friend, who ran his business out of Salford.

The evening passed pleasantly enough and finally the men began to head to the cloakroom to retrieve their coats and hats. Saying his goodbyes to Rudge, Wingood finally made his way over to his parked Jag.

"Hold on Wingood!"

Wingood turned to see a tall grey-haired man waving at him. He paused expectantly, recognising Alex Carruthers, the lodge's Senior Warden.

The older man walked across the tarmac of the car park,

somewhat unsteadily Wingood noticed, and shook Wingood's hand warmly.

"Sorry Clive, I just wanted a quick word, I didn't manage to come over and have a chat earlier."

Wingood looked at him expectantly, Carruthers was clearly a little tipsy and he assumed the man needed a lift home.

"Yes Alex, what's up? Need a lift?"

"No, no, thank you, Jones is giving me a lift," Carruthers said, vaguely pointing back across the car park to where a Cortina sat with its engine idling.

Then he suddenly drew closer, so that Wingood could smell the whisky on his breath.

"I... erm, I just wanted to say that your efforts in helping to organise the forthcoming commemorative anniversary event have been exemplary. You really are a credit to the lodge old man."

Wingood looked at him a little bemused.

"Well thank you Alex, that means a great deal to me."

Carruthers nodded then looked back over his shoulder to where his car was waiting.

"There is something else..." he said turning back to Wingood.

Carruthers hesitated, as if considering his words carefully. Then, in a softer voice, he continued.

"I shouldn't really say this, but you really are a good chap, so I think it's only fair."

Carruthers looked over his shoulder as if suddenly concerned that someone might overhear him.

"That house you sold to that German," he began turning once more to Wingood, "I know it's not strictly on my patch, but as a police Superintendent I do hear all the news you know."

Wingood paused, a sudden, unpleasant chill running down his spine.

"Yes," he answered at length, "What of it Alex?"

Carruthers hesitated before continuing.

"It's a strange one and no mistake..."

The man steadied himself on Wingood's car, then, leaning in towards Wingood, he spoke in a hoarse whisper.

"He disappeared without a trace you know. There was no sign of him, the dog handlers went all over that place, the woods, everywhere. Nothing. Once the investigation had established that he had not lived in the house itself, the police then conducted a sweep of all likely local hotels. At last, it was discovered that one local inn, the White Horse in Alverley, had had a foreign guest fitting von Hallerstein's description. The guest had signed the register as 'Schmidt'. But 'Schmidt' had checked out before Christmas, paying in cash and leaving no forwarding address. By this point the story had hit the national press of course. All the airports and ports were watched for a couple of weeks, even Interpol became involved. But there was still no body, either living or dead, just a little... blood."

"Blood?" Wingood echoed, nonplussed now.

Carruthers leaned even closer, almost conspiratorially, staggering slightly as he did so.

"Yes, a rum thing. It seems that that fellow had

opened up some old well or some such in the cellar of the house. They had to lower the photographer and the investigating officers down on ropes, you know, to see what was what. There's a bloody room down there or some sort of a big cave... A chamber of some kind. That's where they found the blood, a small splatter of dried drops, that turned out to be human blood, enough to show *something* had happened, but the patterning was not consistent with a fall or a blow. However, the lab boys were able to determine that the blood sample was a match for von Hallerstein's type. But there was no body, and no other way out."

He stared now somewhat blearily at Wingood.

"He had chalked some kind of a circle on the floor..." Carruthers suddenly hiccoughed. "Excuse me..." The older man swallowed before continuing. "There were candles and whatnot... Looked like black magic... But nothing else at all. Strange that, eh Clive? Queer thing is there was no trace of blood in the cellar above or even on the walls of the well. The forensic chaps went through that place pretty thoroughly. No, it was as if he had just bled out a little down there, and then vanished into thin air..."

Wingood started as Carruthers leaned forward and grasped Wingood's arm.

"Watch out for MacDonald," he hissed. "He's not one of us, and he's as keen as mustard..."

Then Carruthers winked and tapped his nose knowingly before taking Wingood's hand and shaking it warmly.

"Good night Clive," he said, and before the dazed

Wingood could think to respond, the other man had already walked away.

Wingood watched as Carruthers wandered waveringly back to the waiting Cortina. Somewhat dazedly, he remained standing there long after the Cortina's taillights had faded away into the night gloom. As the drizzle turned into rain, the realisation had finally dawned on his dulled mind. Wingood might very well be a suspect in the business of von Hallerstein's disappearance. For several seconds he attempted to rationalise things and supress the idea as a simple absurdity. After all, Carruthers had clearly had too much to drink. Nor had the policeman said anything directly indicating that Wingood was under suspicion. Wingood assured himself that he was clearly overreacting. But he remembered too, the hard stare inspector MacDonald had given him at the end of their brief interview, and Carruthers admonition to be wary of the detective inspector.

Shuddering, Wingood pushed his hand into his coat pocket and rummaged for the car keys feeling suddenly depressed. Finally, as the rain began to trickle down into his collar, he climbed into his Jag and drove home.

CHAPTER THREE
ANTROBUS

That night, Wingood had his second nightmare about Marchley Howe. The details of his dream eluded him once more, but when he finally awoke in the grey hours of the early morning, he was both tired and agitated. Sighing, he shuffled to the bathroom and ran himself a bath. Whilst he shaved, he looked mournfully at his reflection in the bathroom mirror. Dark lines were now forming under his eyes. He knew that he needed to find some kind of resolution if only for his own piece of mind. He needed to exorcise the thought of Marchley Howe from his psyche once and for all! Damn that German and his weirdness, he thought. But what to do? What to do indeed.

After dressing he made a pot of tea and took a cup up to Doris who was still snoring gently. Quietly placing the cup and saucer on the bedside table beside her, Wingood looked out of the bedroom window as he absently adjusted the knot of his tie. Out there he saw only the banal normality of ordinary solid houses and the small, tidy rear gardens of their quiet suburban neighbourhood.

His mind drifted back to another time in what now seemed like another life, so many years before, so far away. Wingood had been little more than a boy. Yet the memory was still vivid. There he had been, lying amongst the barren rocks and drifting sands of the desert, surrounded by the noise and thunder of artillery, hiding from the creaking, metallic screech of the tanks, terrified by the shouts and screams of dying men. The battle had raged all about him and he had felt crushed by an overwhelming horror. Huddled in a shell hole, it was not long before Wingood had been joined by another soldier, an Australian N.C.O. who was himself desperately scrambling for cover from the line of fire. The man took the measure of the cowering young private, his eyes glancing to the rifle lying on the ground where it had been discarded. Then, jumping forwards, the corporal had gripped Wingood's arm and shaken him roughly. But the firm words that followed were meant kindly.

"There's no help in being a cry baby son. You're in the middle of a great big pile of shit." Still gripping Wingood's arm, the Australian craned his neck to see through the dust and smoke that swirled all around them. He ducked involuntarily at the nearby crump of an exploding shell. Turning back to Wingood he smiled. "It's time to look death in the eye and give him the bloody forks."

He formed a 'V' with the index and middle finger of his

left hand, then aggressively gestured in the direction of the German guns.

"Otherwise, you'll end up mad or runnin' from the devil all your life... Now pick up that bloody gun and get ready."

Wingood had roughly wiped the tears and snot from his face. Then, biting his lip, he had reached for his rifle. The two were quickly separated in the ensuing chaos and he had never seen the corporal again. But the man's words had remained with him.

Wingood would return to Marchley Howe. He would face his phantoms and clear his mind in order to allow prosaic reality to reassert itself and to set things to rest. He would go and 'give it the forks'. All he need do was take a quick, surreptitious examination of the house and, he felt sure, all would be put back into perspective. Wingood glanced at his watch. There was no time like the present and it was still very early. The Saturday morning roads would be quiet. He no longer had the key in the safe at work, he assumed the police would have returned to lock the house or at the very least have padlocked the door, but that would be no problem. He had a tire iron in his boot, it would be easy enough to carefully prize open one of the old windows at the back of the house. Wingood could be there and back before Debbie opened the estate agency at nine. Shivering slightly, partly in fear, partly with an almost juvenile excitement, he quietly left the house before he could change his mind.

The drive was, as anticipated, completed relatively quickly and the roads were indeed quiet enough. However, when Wingood finally pulled up before what now seemed to him to be the rather ominous gates of Marchley Howe, he was already beginning to have second thoughts. The gates were closed but unlocked. For some minutes Wingood sat in his car and stared at them indecisively. Finally, steeling himself, he climbed out of the car and pushed them open. After driving the Jag through, Wingood stopped once more and quickly closed the gates after him. In the unlikely event that somebody should pass along the quiet, adjoining lane, Wingood reasoned, the closed gates would raise no suspicions. Before he could change his mind, he accelerated along the track and left the gates far behind him.

It was turning into a fine day, and Wingood was sharply reminded of the day of the viewing when he had awaited the unfortunate von Hallerstein. Today however, the woods were leafy and green, and wildflowers carpeted the meadows beyond the mature woodlands. As the house came into view it looked just as he had last seen it, old and beautiful. Wingood frowned, von Hallerstein must have had a screw loose whatever had happened to him he concluded. Still, it would do him good to look over things once more. Besides, there was the decidedly uncomfortable possibility (however slight it might be) that the house might very well remain in his business portfolio. Despite his own conclusions about von Hallerstein's soundness of mind, he had no idea whether von Hallerstein had even had any family, and, after all, von Hallerstein had effectively gifted it back to him, the letter was clear in that regard at least. Although von Hallerstein had made some outlandish claims (along with some weird and eccentric warnings), Wingood realised that he *could*, just possibly, be responsible for selling the house all over again. Perhaps, he considered, if that were indeed the final resolution, he should concentrate this time on the American market...

Lost in these somewhat vague and fanciful musings he drove the Jag quickly across the parkland towards the looming house. However, this time, instead of drawing up on the drive at the front of the house, he passed the door slowly, confirming his suspicions about the locked door as he glanced at the new and shiny padlock and chain that hung in place there. Wingood passed on and slipped the car into the cobbled and walled yard that contained the stable blocks and other outbuildings set back at the left-hand side of the property. He brought the Jag to a stop and killed the engine. Sitting for some moments in the impressive rural silence, broken only by birdsong, he stared at the imposing rear of the house, quietly remembering all that he knew about von Hallerstein's mysterious activities and ultimate disappearance. He remembered too the facts he had discovered about the strange history of the house and the site itself, of the monks and the saintly Albin, of the dark conspiracies of Venables and the links to missing children. He hesitated again then, wondering what he really hoped to achieve by coming back. What's more, he starkly reminded himself, his return was contrary to the express wishes of both von Hallerstein *and* the police.

Pushing these uncomfortable thoughts out of his mind, Wingood climbed out of the car and walked across the cobbled yard. He unlatched an old door in a high brick wall and found himself in the remains of what had once been the walled kitchen garden. Pushing gingerly through the half open wooden door, he made his way forwards through newly green nettles and came at last to the back of the house. He looked up at the sightless windows and, suppressed an involuntary shudder. Taking a deep breath, Wingood looked through the nearest thick-paned, leaded window. In the dim interior he could see a bare empty room with a small dark, cheerless fireplace. Wingood recognised the room as the butler's pantry. He studied the old wood of the window frame carefully for a moment.

Then, turning quickly, he returned to the car and, after rummaging for a moment in his boot, pulled out a chrome tyre-iron. Wingood hefted the heavy metal tool boldly but as his eyes rested once more on the house, he could not prevent another shiver passing up his spine.

"Ridiculous," he chided himself aloud. "Get a grip Wingood!"

Straightening up, the estate agent popped his torch into his jacket pocket and, after closing the boot, quickly made his way back to the window. He looked inside again. Something small and dark tapped the inside of the glass. Wingood jumped then squinted. It was just a blue-bottle fly, bashing stupidly at the window in a vain effort to escape. Smiling weakly at his own temerity, Wingood lifted the tyre iron and fitted the sharp flat end between the frame and the window itself. He was relieved when the window opened easily with only the minimum amount of split wood as the ancient catch provided no resistance. Wingood carefully levered the wood apart. As he pulled the window open widely, he suddenly stepped back as a cloud of black flies rose buzzing out of the aperture towards him. Wingood ineffectually waved his hand at them as they flew out of the open window. Then, grimacing in disgust, he brushed away a thin line of twitching and dead flies that still littered the interior sill. Once his way was cleared, Wingood stepped onto a large and cracked ceramic pot and then, with some effort, slowly pulled himself up onto the window ledge. Grumbling at his discomfort, he carefully lowered himself down onto the bare, red-tiled floor below and dusted himself off.

Looking about him, Wingood took a deep measured breath in an attempt to slow his now rapidly beating heart. Then, moving briskly, he opened the dark heavy door of the pantry and stepped out into the corridor beyond. He reminded himself that he had walked the passages and rooms of this house many times over the years and had never felt anything 'unpleasant'. Nor was it any different today. Despite his own jumpiness and the now fading memory of his nightmare, the house felt solidly ordinary and, what's more, beautifully picturesque. He paused briefly and opened a storage cupboard at the end of the corridor. Flicking on his torch he illuminated the old electric meter and saw from the slow tick of the dial that the electricity was still connected. That was good, despite his nervousness, he thought that he should at least peer into the cellar.

Closing the cupboard, Wingood made his way through

the echoing kitchen and soon left the service areas behind him, finally entering the wooden panelled entrance hall. Bright sunlight flickered in colourful beams through the stained-glass windows just as it had on the day that von Hallerstein had viewed the property. Nothing indeed had changed so far as he could see. Suddenly curious, he walked into the Great Hall and looked about him. But the room was now completely empty, the fold up chair and other miscellaneous items that the handyman Latchwood had seen there, were gone. Returning to the entrance hall, Wingood climbed the broad wooden stairs and quietly explored the upper stories. All the rooms were empty and just as he had remembered them. Satisfied, Wingood retraced his steps back to the entrance hall. At last, he looked at the arched cellar door. He did not relish exploring the cellar, but his curiosity was still piqued. Besides, he wanted to see the lighting installation that Latchwood and his apprentice had installed. Wingood slowly opened the heavy door and peered into the darkness that seemed now to lap at the top of the old worn steps. Once again, he flicked on his torch and, leaning cautiously into the dark space, shone it about. To his left he saw what he was looking for, a new, large metal switch that was mounted to the bare stone wall just inside the entrance.

The switch was linked to a thick cable that ran down the wall and faded into the darkness. Holding his breath, Wingood reached over and flicked the switch on. The sudden burst of brightness was startling. Quickly descending the stairs in amazement, he finally stepped out into the open space of the cellar itself and stared about him.

It was just as Latchwood had described it. The once dark and dismal space was now starkly illuminated by a series of bright halogen flood lights, fixed at intervals to the walls and cunningly positioned so that even the darkest corners were lit by their artificial radiance. Blinking but emboldened by the excessive light of the lamps, Wingood belatedly turned off his torch and looked about him again. He noted the large heavy bulk of a diesel generator, standing in the far-left hand corner of the cellar and surrounded by several drums of what Wingood assumed must be its fuel. Turning back to the open space before him he made his way across the worn stone flags of the floor towards a large arch in the farthest wall. The second chamber was as brightly illuminated as the first though it was a smaller space, circular and empty. Several smaller antechambers led from this space but though each was similarly lit, each was empty and none offered anything of interest to see. However, it was the larger space that lay beyond the second chamber that now drew Wingood's attention. As he passed through the next archway, he felt his heart begin to beat more rapidly. There, just as had been described to him, was the dark entrance to the pit. There were no other exits from this wide, square chamber. A heap of broken flagstones and thick, rotted wooden beams, were piled to one side, but Wingood's gaze was fixed on the expansive dark circle of the well. Despite the incandescence of the halogen lamps, the light did not reach far into the inky black depths. The trembling in his legs irked him, but very slowly, Wingood approached the nearest edge and looked cautiously down.

And then the lights went out.

Plunged into a sudden impenetrable darkness, Wingood let out a shout of terror. He desperately fumbled in his jacket pocket for the torch. As he shakily clicked the thin beam on, he stopped, straining his senses. Had he heard something? He shone the torch about him unnerved by the dancing shadows and the horrible proximity of the pit at his feet. Yes! There it was again. The sound seemed to come as if from a great distance. An eerie but oh, so faint whistling, a dreadful, piping whine. And now he realised that the noise was unquestionably coming from the chasm below. Shining the light of the torch back to the edge of the dark hole beneath him, Wingood backed quickly away. There it was again! And there was now something else. A draft, weak but just discernible, touched his face. And the current of air brought with it a rank odour. Wingood's nose wrinkled as he continued to back away from the foetid air rising from the pit. Then he heard yet another sound, and despite his sudden desire to be gone, to regain the fresh air and sunlight of the spring day somewhere far above, he hesitated, frozen beneath the high stone arch entrance to the chamber, straining once more to hear.

It sounded like a slow, dragging, shuffling...

At that, Wingood at last turned and fled, now desperate to reach the stairs and regain the sanity of the daylight. But in his chaotic flight, he collided with one of the many stone pillars of the undercroft. Suddenly seeing stars and swearing now with both fear and pain, he righted himself and then dashed once more, each moment expecting something to reach for his heels in the dark. Somehow, he found his way, though he had now lost his torch. Clambering and lurching up the stone stairs, Wingood fell out of the cellar entrance and frantically slammed the heavy wooden door shut behind him, turning the key in the lock. Leaning his back against the door he slid down to the floor, his face white with shock, a thin stream of blood dripping from his nose onto his shirt. He was breathing heavily, his heart hammering dangerously in his chest. But he heard the strange piping sound once more, and it seemed nearer now though muffled by the thickness of the wooden door. With a gasp of horror, Wingood scrambled to his feet and fled.

Wingood had little memory of his flight from the house and when at last he finally came back to his senses, he found himself sitting in his car some miles away at a petrol station. He looked at his still ashen face in the rear-view mirror and then, wincing, he tried to wipe the dried blood from his now bruised features with his handkerchief. Looking out of the window he saw a telephone box and then glanced at his watch. It was past nine now. Wingood's hands were still shaking, and he could not make any sense of what had happened in the cellar of Marchley Howe. His shame at his fear was only slightly assuaged by the memory of the terror he had felt. It *had* been real. He was not dreaming. There was something... He quickly cut off such thoughts and reached into his pocket for change. Getting out of the car, he proceeded across the road to the bright red phone box.

"Hello? Debbie? It's Clive...er Mr. Wingood. I've had a..." Wingood hesitated for a moment and took a deep breath.

"Erm... I've had a spot of bother with the car and I'm afraid I may be a little late."

In the end, the lie came surprisingly easily, but Wingood felt no embarrassment, only a desperate need to somehow regain control, to *normalise* things.

"No, don't worry, I have everything in hand. There aren't any appointments this morning are there? No? Good. There's nothing else that I can't catch up with later. Can you hold the fort until I can get there...? Could you? Yes, yes, I'm fine. Thank you, Debbie, I do appreciate it and I'll see you soon."

He sighed as he replaced the receiver and stared at the petrol station across the road where his car was parked. Slowly, he walked back across the road and entered the shop. Seeing the blood on Wingood's shirt and the purpling bruise across the bridge of his nose, the short man behind the counter gave him a queer look.

"Are you alright mate?" he asked uneasily.

But Wingood offered no explanation. His mind still racing, he bought a packet of Players cigarettes and a box of matches then returned to the car and began to smoke. He stared out of the windscreen, idly watching the glint of a far-off aeroplane as it began its approach to Speke airport on the other side of the distant Mersey. He had shakily smoked two more cigarettes before he had a sudden, desperate idea. Wingood fumbled in his pocket and drew out the remaining change. Habitually, he looked at his watch before walking back across the road.

Entering the phone box, he opened the tattered directory. In a few moments he had found a likely name and number. Wingood ran his fingers through his thinning hair nervously hesitating, then he picked up the receiver and dialled the number. The phone rang for some moments until finally somebody answered. Wingood took two pence and quickly put it in the slot.

"Hello? Is that Mr. Antrobus? Mr. Jack Antrobus the writer?"

There was a moment's silence at the other end of the telephone line.

"Aye, who's this?" a man's voice, an old gravelly northern voice, slow and deliberate.

Wingood cleared his throat.

"Ah, Mr. Antrobus, my name is Clive Wingood, I'm an estate agent from Netherton. I was wondering..."

"No thank you, I'm not interested."

Before Wingood could protest, there was a click, and the line went dead.

Wingood swore and felt in his pocket for more change. He dialled the number again.

"Hello?"

"Ah, hello Mr. Antrobus, it's Clive Wingood again, please let me..."

"I told you already, I'm not interested."

"Marchley Howe!" Wingood cried desperately.

The line went suddenly quiet.

At first Wingood thought Antrobus had hung up again. Then he heard the other man sigh.

"Marchley Howe? What about it? Is this to do with that missing Jerry?"

The phone pips sounded and Wingood fumbled a ten pence piece into the slot.

"Hello?" Antrobus said.

Wingood sighed in relief.

"Yes, I'm here Mr. Antrobus. I... I need your help. I was... I was the estate agent that sold the property."

"Well?" Antrobus demanded gruffly.

Wingood swallowed nervously.

"You see, I've read your book. I've read 'Our Mysterious County', that's why I called *you*. Could we meet, perhaps have a cup of tea and a chat? I don't want to talk on the phone... It's just... Please Mr. Antrobus?"

There was a further silence. Seconds ticked by.

Wingood had now run out of change for the phone.

"Aye, alright," Antrobus at last replied somewhat grumpily. "But you'd better be what you say you are..."

There was a further pause, Wingood could hear the man's steady breathing on the other end of the line.

Finally, Antrobus spoke again.

"Well, you've got my number, so I assume you 'ave my address from the phone book?"

Wingood looked at the open phonebook perched on top of the payphone.

"Yes, I've got it," he said.

"Alright. Then come to my house tomorrow at two. Just head south towards Mara Wood on the B road. Once you've passed through the forest, take the first righthand lane marked Eddesbury. The entrance to my property is on your left, about a mile from the turn off. There's a white-painted wooden gate marked Shippen Farm. Drive slowly down my lane, I have chickens. I'll make sure to put the kettle on."

And with that closing remark, Antrobus abruptly hung up.

Wingood replaced the receiver and took a sharp intake of breath. Taking a pencil and a notepad from his jacket pocket, he jotted down the address then left the phone box.

When Wingood walked through the door of the estate agency, Debbie had been clearly shaken by his bloodied and dishevelled appearance. He had hastily explained that his injury was simply the result of having had to break sharply to avoid a dog and, unfortunately, he had forgotten to fasten his seatbelt. Despite her evident shock, Debbie at least appeared to accept the explanation that Wingood's bruised and pallid features were due to a sudden collision with his steering wheel, but she nevertheless insisted that Wingood should go straight home and rest. Still dazed and very shaken from his experience at Marchley Howe, Wingood was in fact only too glad to comply.

Debbie smiled comfortingly but she was unable to hide the concern in her voice.

"Get yourself off Mr. Wingood, I'll lock up."

Wingood nodded wanly. Finally, after making a cursory attempt to look at the mail, he thanked Debbie and left the premises.

He drove home slowly. Mercifully, Doris was out. Kicking off his shoes, Wingood poured himself a stiff drink (after guiltily checking the clock to ensure that it was now past noon) and retired to bed after taking some aspirin and one of Doris's sleeping tablets. With the curtains drawn against the brightness of the day, he lay for some minutes on the large bed, wondering if he was indeed losing his mind. As the soporific drug began to take effect, he felt himself slowly retreating into a soft and warm fuzziness whilst, simultaneously, his desperate attempts at rationalisation evaporated into nothingness.

Wingood awoke the next morning with a start. He looked down at his shirt and seeing the dark bloody stain, remembered. He had slept right through the night. Startled, he looked about the room then somewhat stiffly, he stood up.

"Doris," he called. "Doris!"

He walked over to the top of the stairs.

"Doris?"

There was a sound downstairs followed by a familiar, exasperated response.

"I'm busy."

Wingood frowned at the crabby tone of his wife's voice.

"I had an accident yesterday dear," he called out. "I'm fine but I had a bump on my nose and a frightful headache."

A quiet grunt from the kitchen.

"I've already heard. That girl from the office phoned last night to see how you were. And don't expect me to be able to wash the blood off your shirt."

Wingood sighed.

"Well dear, I have an appointment at two so I'm just going to have a bath and clean myself up a bit."

Wingood spent a long time lying in a hot, deep bath desperately trying to relax, but the turmoil in his mind would not abate.

He was glad to leave Doris and the house behind him. She was in one of her moods. But more than this, Wingood felt a desperate need to find answers. He felt as if he might literally be going mad.

It was another fine day. The road south was busy with the cars of Sunday day-trippers, people escaping from the urban sprawl on the far side of the Mersey. The next day was the new Bank Holiday Monday, but rain had been forecast for May Day itself, and people were seemingly making the most of the current fine weather. As his Jag glided through Mara Forest, he saw families picnicking and children gripping rapidly melting ice creams. As Wingood navigated past the numerous ice-cream vans, hotdog vendors and parked cars, that lined the edge of the picnic spots, he was reminded how remote that sane and normal world now seemed to him. His mood was dark by the time he finally passed through the southern boundary of the forest. The day seemed glaringly bright after the verdant light of the fast-retreating trees. Squinting, Wingood soon saw a small, rapidly approaching road sign. The marker stated - *Eddesbury, 2 miles*. Wingood slowed his Jag and turned right into the narrow lane. Hoping he would not meet any oncoming cars or tractors along the single-track road, Wingood accelerated slowly.

He found Shippen Farm as easily as Antrobus had described it. The gate looked freshly painted and the track beyond was lined on each side with a border of brightly coloured wildflowers. Wingood opened the gate and drove through, pausing only to dutifully close the gate after himself. Then he drove slowly along the track, carefully reminding himself to be on the lookout for chickens. The hedge on either side now reached right up over the track. The entanglement of the greenery overhead formed a cool, leafy tunnel. Then the car suddenly emerged into a bright and sunny cobbled yard.

The old thatched and timber framed farmhouse that now filled the view before him, seemed to be as venerable as Marchley Howe itself, but Wingood preferred this simpler rural picture. It was, he reflected, as pretty as a chocolate box scene. Turning off his engine, Wingood stepped out into the warm sunshine and watched the clucking chickens strut busily about the yard. The fowls pecked and scratched at the floor incessantly, seemingly unperturbed by Wingood's presence.

Wingood was jolted out of this reverie by the opening of the low farmhouse door. A grizzled man dressed in a baggy old cardigan now glared at him from the doorway.

"Mr. Antrobus?" he ventured.

Wingood stared at the man uncertainly. The old, but hale looking man, stepped out into the yard and straightened up. He placed his hands on his hips and regarded Wingood sharply in return.

After some moments, he finally nodded.

"Aye, I'm Antrobus."

He stared at the estate agent with what Wingood now saw, were startlingly bright, blue eyes.

Antrobus looked at Wingood's now proffered hand. Then the two men shook hands formally and Antrobus motioned Wingood inside.

"Shippen Farm, that's an unusual name," Wingood offered smiling, assuming his usual air when entering a new property. He walked over the threshold and looked about him appraisingly. He was proud of his 'ice breakers'.

The hall was broad, dark oak beams crossed the ceiling just above head height. A wide, bare wooden staircase rose on the righthand side. The uncarpeted floor was made of huge slabs of age-worn sandstone. It all looked very old, but well kept.

"Is it nautical?" he asked turning to Antrobus.

Antrobus paused and looked at Wingood then, shaking his head incredulously.

"Eh, you what? Nautical? In the middle of the countryside? No, it's not *nautical*, it's an Old English word for cowshed. And it's not for sale neither."

Before the now flummoxed Wingood could respond Antrobus waved his arm at him.

"Come on, I've got the kettle on."

The old man led the somewhat abashed Wingood through the hall into a large sitting room of sorts.

"Have a seat 'ere," he said pointing towards two highbacked fireside chairs. The chairs flanked an old wood burner stove, but the fire was not lit, and despite the warmth of the day outside, the room remained cool.

"Hang on for a minute," the older man said. Antrobus turned and left the room. This was soon followed by sounds of clanking from what Wingood assumed was the kitchen.

Wingood looked about him. The room was a good size, but it was crammed with books and huge, tottering piles of magazines. Laden bookshelves lined the walls and there were books in heaps on occasional tables. Several heavy volumes lay scattered about the floor at the foot of the other fireside chair. To the left of the hearth was a large writing desk that stood in front of a tall narrow window. Sitting room come study, Wingood decided.

Unlike the rest of the room, the broad expanse of the desk's shiny, wooden surface was bare save for three objects. The dominant one was an impressive gunmetal coloured typewriter marked 'Royal Quiet Deluxe'. Beside it, was a rather battered looking paraffin lamp. The third object was a photograph, a portrait of a young woman standing next to a haystack and laughing. The faded, sepia picture was held in an old silver frame, lovingly polished.

His musings were interrupted when Antrobus, carrying a large tray, re-entered the room. He placed the tray on a small, ornately carved tea table.

"Sugar?" he asked.

Wingood nodded.

"Yes, two please."

Antrobus poured the tea and added two heaped spoons

of sugar before passing the cup and saucer to Wingood. He then settled himself in the other chair.

"You can call me Jack," he said at length.

Wingood nodded relaxing a little and smiled.

"My name's Clive. Thank you again for agreeing to see me today Mr. Antrobus... er, Jack."

"Aye, well, I get fed up of talking to the chickens," Antrobus replied archly. "Now then, what can I do for you?"

Wingood smiled weakly as Antrobus, now sipping at his tea, continued to stare at him.

"As I said on the phone yesterday, I was the estate agent that sold Marchley Howe..." he paused and began to unconsciously bite at his fingernails. "I think something is *wrong* with the house, but I don't know what, nor what I should do." There was suddenly a pleading tone to his voice.

Antrobus placed his own cup and saucer on the tray and leaned forwards.

"What do you think I can do?" he asked bluntly.

Wingood raised his eyes to look at Antrobus.

"You know about this sort of thing, you've written about... things like this... and you know about Marchley Howe." Wingood faltered and fell silent once more.

Antrobus nodded.

"Yes, I do, and I might 'ave my own ideas. But first, I want you to tell me your story... from the beginning."

Haltingly, Wingood began to narrate the story of the sale and von Hallerstein's odd behaviour during the viewing of the house itself. He told Antrobus about the mysterious letter he had received from von Hallerstein and then the disturbing encounter with Carruthers after the Masonic meeting. As Wingood talked, Antrobus said nothing but at least seemed to be listening intently. Finally, Wingood reluctantly told him about his return to Marchley Howe yesterday morning. As he recounted the incident, he felt uneasy once more. When he had finished, Wingood lapsed into silence and stared into his now empty teacup.

"How about another pot of tea? I forgot to put on the tea cosy and this one's gone cold" Antrobus suggested, as he touched the side of the pot.

Before Wingood could reply, the sprightly Antrobus was already up with the laden tray in his hands.

"Come on, I want to show you summat."

Bemused, Wingood stood up and followed the older man out of the room.

Antrobus strode ahead, past the steeply climbing hall stairs, down the oak-panelled corridor towards the bright kitchen that lay before him. But he paused before entering it and, setting the tray down, he reached up to pluck a large, leatherbound volume from a shelf above his head.

Turning, Antrobus handed it to Wingood, and said:

"It's eighteenth century, so be careful with it,"

He watched as Wingood opened the heavy book.

"It was written and self-published in 1780 by a county antiquarian called Jonathan Bowden, it's a collection of folktales and the like that he gathered together on his travels around the countryside. There's no mention of Venables in this book - I suppose Bowden thought Venables' recent skulduggery outside of the scope of his treatise - but you know *that* story *if* you've read my book... No, it's not about Venables, but it is about Marchley Howe and it's an older story. Go to the bookmarked page, there's a picture there..."

Wingood leafed through the volume to find the desired page.

"It's a mezzotint," Antrobus explained. "Just look at that fine detail."

Wingood squinted then reached into his pocket for his reading glasses.

He looked at the image sceptically at first, wondering what on earth Antrobus wanted him to see. Then, as his eyes focused on the picture, he took a sharp intake of breath.

"It's Marchley Howe!" he exclaimed, shivering now as he recognised the familiar architecture of the old house in the image. He was drawn to how concurrent it looked to his own mental image of the house, just as if the artist had etched the image only recently. Nothing seemed to have changed. But Wingood's gaze was quickly drawn to the cloaked figure in the centre of the frame, standing arms raised, facing the front of the house, his back to the viewer. To Wingood's eye the house looked as if it were on fire, but he could see no representation of flames, only a dark and oily blackness that billowed like smoke out of the building itself. In the sky above, rode a pale thin crescent disk that Wingood assumed was the moon.

Then, slowly, he read the copperplate inscription below the image.

. . .

'Dr. Dee and the Great Warding of the Dark', 25th February 1598, shewn at the time of the Full Eclypse.

"The artist could have just used the house as his model. After all, the book was written in 1780, that's nearly two hundred years later!"

Antrobus pointed at the figure before the house.

"See who that is? That's John Dee. There's only a short paragraph about it, read it out loud. Look there," he pointed a gnarled finger at the text. "It's underlined faintly in pencil. I'll put the kettle back on."

Collecting the tray, Antrobus walked into the kitchen and Wingood heard the clank of the kettle going onto the kitchen range.

He looked back at the text and felt suddenly self-conscious.

"Erm..."

Wingood cleared his throat before he began to read aloud.

"*There is a popular legend sustained in the oral tradition from the north of the county... that tells how the Warden of Christ's College, Manchester, the Queen's conjurer himself, Dr. John Dee, was called to serve God and banish a dark evil that had taken form and possession of a noble house. According to the legend, Dee travelled to Marchley Howe before the full eclipse, fearing that the very Devil himself might peer into our world unabashed by the light of the Lord's sun. Using certain words and signs revealed to him by the angels of the Almighty himself,*

Dr. Dee was able to seal the dark and stop its entry into our world."

As Wingood concluded reading, Antrobus reappeared with the tray.

"Right, well, come on then, put the book back up there on the shelf."

Obeying dumbly, Wingood replaced the book and followed Antrobus back into the sitting room.

When they were seated once more, Antrobus stirred the tea and reached for the strainer.

"Have another cup."

He poured the tea and passed it to Wingood, then, he paused, and frowned before speaking.

"You told me that von Hallerstein had found something in the basement. You said you saw the hole yourself, only yesterday."

Wingood nodded, shivering slightly.

Antrobus continued:

"The Jerry was convinced that this hole was... dangerous, and rather emphatically told you so. And yet you went there and had a look yourself."

Surprisingly, Antrobus chuckled.

"You've got some guts; I'll give you that."

But Wingood shook his head nervously.

"No, it certainly wasn't bravery. Quite the opposite really. I just wanted to exorcise that uncomfortable feeling I've had for months now... I thought that if I went back and saw that there was nothing to it, then everything would return to normal..."

Antrobus stirred his tea.

"But you didn't find 'normality' there did you? You encountered *something* down there... Something that gave you a bit of a turn."

Antrobus reached into his pocket and pulled out an old briar pipe. In silence he filled the bowl carefully with tobacco and lit a match. After filling the air with a pungent cloud of smoke, he pointed the stem of the pipe at Wingood.

"Did you know that the founders of the priory, those Hospitallers, were no ordinary monks? They were a *military* religious order. So, what were they doing setting up a priory in the backwaters of rural England, eh? And why did Robert of Deva mention them in a book he'd translated about spirits and demonology?"

Wingood shook his head.

"I don't quite understand... er... Jack."

Antrobus tamped and relit his pipe before continuing.

"Don't you see? It seems to me that that 'well' predates the house *and* the priory. That's why there's a legend about St. Albin and his cleansing of the 'heathens' in that very area."

He pulled on his pipe before continuing.

"It was all forest then of course, Mara Forest in fact, but it wasn't always some tended playground for weekend townies. No, not then."

He shook his head and drew on his pipe.

"In the old days it stretched right across the county, from mountain wall in the Celtic west to mountain wall in the Danish east. It took a long time for Christianity to penetrate either the forest or the hearts of those who lived within the forest's fastness. Celts, Romans, Vikings and Anglo-Saxons... I reckon they all knew of that site. As for the monks, they came to watch it, to *guard* it."

He peered at Wingood keenly.

"In that brief reference, Robert of Deva mentioned something else about them. He said that they had a special Papal warrant from the new pope, Callixtus the second."

Standing quickly, Antrobus walked over to one of the bookshelves and after some moments, withdrew a large book, impressed into the faded red leather of the spine was a gilded crucifix. The old man thumbed through the pages then grunted in satisfaction.

"Here it is..." then Antrobus began to read from the old, foxed pages. "*And so, it was ordered that over diverse lands, knightly monks would find and defeat Satan's agents here on earth...*

"Then the book goes on to list the orders created or chosen," Antrobus said, now looking up at Wingood. "They were sent all over the place or at least wherever the church held sway...." He squinted as he returned his gaze to the book. "And here are our lot... the Hospitaller Brotherhood of St. Patroclus..." Antrobus paused dramatically and stared at Wingood. "Known as... the Wards of the *Black Worm*." He replaced the book on the shelf. "You don't need to be a rocket scientist to work it out Clive."

Wingood smiled wanly.

"Well, I'm not quite sure I follow your meaning..."

Antrobus puffed on the pipe once more and seemed to be considering his words carefully.

"Now, I've not seen this 'well', but based on von Hallerstein's description..." he paused. "You said he mentioned summat about Andean ruins?"

Wingood nodded dumbly.

"Aye, well," Antrobus continued, "my guess is that this hole is very old indeed, maybe even Atlantean... but I'd need to see it first to say properly."

Wingood took a sharp intake of breath and then, half-laughing, half incredulous, exclaimed:

"Atlantean, like Atlantis?! Well really... I don't see how..."

Antrobus frowned and pointed the pipe stem again.

"Clive, you've got to start thinking beyond the pages of the *Reader's Digest* and the propaganda they pump out of the ruddy telly. Yes, bloody Atlantis!"

Wingood shook his head then drained his cup of tea.

"Alright... Jack..." he began, his head had begun to ache, and he rubbed his palms against his temples. "But what about von Hallerstein? What on earth do you think happened to him?"

Wingood now looked at Antrobus almost pleadingly.

But the older man only shrugged and drew on his pipe before replying.

"Well, for a start I reckon von Hallerstein got the date wrong. Whatever he was up to in my book his efforts were doomed from the start. He seems to have been convinced that the winter solstice was critical, but I don't think that it was."

Antrobus looked at Wingood's puzzled face. The estate agent was clearly finding this all very difficult to process.

"Think on that picture in Bowden's book, the 'Great Warding of the Dark'? That happened during an eclipse."

Suddenly bending down, Antrobus quickly pulled a 'Farmer's Almanac' out from beneath his chair.

"Let's just have a look 'ere." He frowned as he flicked through the calendar and then held up a page triumphantly for Wingood to see.

"Look 'ere, twenty-first of June 1978, that's just fifty-one days from now, it's the summer solstice, but *look*..."

Wingood put on his glasses and stared at the symbol Antrobus was tapping excitedly.

"Eh?" Wingood grunted, nonplussed.

"The eclipse!" Antrobus exclaimed. "The bloody eclipse, that *must* be the date. It's a total eclipse on the summer solstice. That's about as dire as it gets."

Antrobus reached across and gripped Wingood's arm making the other man jump.

"These late eclipses in the sun and moon portend no good to us..."

Letting go of Wingood's arm, he tapped the side of his nose with the end of his pipe.

"Now I'm sure the Jerry got the date wrong... He went down there with a purpose, to do something... By your own account you heard, smelt and *felt* something. So, whatever the Jerry tried to do must 'ave failed. And now he's gone... But he may have made matters worse. For a start he opened the well, then he probably made contact... Happen he has done summat that was best left alone."

Wingood blinked and was still clearly bewildered.

"Come on Clive, let's go for a walk," Antrobus suggested, seemingly spontaneously. "Rain's coming in again later, but it's still a while away."

And so, without further ado, Antrobus ushered Wingood out of the room. Following Antrobus out of the backdoor, he found himself in a large vegetable garden. The old man led Wingood past the burgeoning beds of vegetables and then past a pig stye to a gate. The gate opened into a large field. Wrinkling his nose at the smell of the pigs, Wingood was glad to step out into the grassy meadow beyond. The hawthorns that skirted the rear of the farm were beginning to flower with bee-loud, May blossom, and the sweetness of the woody scent was already strong.

Antrobus had a tall shepherd's staff in his hand and quickly led the way out into the field. He stopped in the middle of the tree-lined meadow and leaned on his staff.

Mopping his now perspiring forehead with his handkerchief, Wingood came up and stood beside him.

"Pretty here, isn't it?" Antrobus remarked eyeing Wingood keenly.

Wingood looked about him. He could see the large green mass of Eddesbury Hill rising and dominating the western horizon. To the north he could make out the green line of Mara Forest. Away to the south rose a ridge of steep hills, starkly contrasting with the regularity of the county's level plain.

"Aye, pretty, and very, very old." Antrobus continued. "Take Castle Ditch for example, yon hill of Eddesbury. A hill fort, over two thousand years old. What stories it might tell, what blood was spilled there?"

Wingood squinted towards the rise and raised his hand to shield his eyes from the westering light of the sun.

"It's an old place our county Clive."

The old man pointed his staff down at Wingood's polished brogue shoes.

"Look down at your feet."

Wingood looked down doubtfully.

"Well?" he said.

Antrobus smiled.

"Beneath the long grass and wildflowers under your feet, down under the deep sod, below the teeth of the plough, is a road."

Wingood frowned.

"A road?"

Antrobus nodded.

"Aye, a Roman road. It passed right through here, running down and through my yard. Like I said, an old country."

Wingood stared back towards the farmhouse before turning back to Antrobus.

"You said that von Hallerstein had made matters worse? What did you mean?"

Antrobus cleared his throat and spat.

"Well, of course, I don't rightly know, except that I don't

think we can just leave things as they are. If I'm right, and the eclipse *is* the day, then we have to act."

Wingood shook his head.

"What does this mean? The eclipse is the date? What date? What, what, what?!"

Wingood had suddenly lost his composure completely and he sat down heavily on the soft grass of the meadow.

Antrobus looked down at him pityingly.

"Alright Clive, humour me just for a moment and trust your own feelings about this. You said that there was something wrong with the house, right? Your Jerry friend knew it to be the case. Let's suppose that he wasn't mad and come to that neither are you. I know *I'm* not."

Antrobus paused to watch a skylark rise out of the meadow and begin singing.

"So, it's like this as I see it," he began, looking back now at Wingood.

"For the sake of argument let's agree that there is something unnatural at Marchley Howe. Something is there under the house, let's call it its old name, the Black Worm. And this presence is down that well, somewhere far below the house. Now, imagine this Black Worm has been there for a long time, if your Jerry was right, maybe *tens* of thousands of years. Once it might have been worshipped as a god, and *fed*... But the land changed, and seas rose and fell. The degenerated descendants of the old race fell far, until they were little more than primitive tribes of forest dwellers who feared hungry gods. Yet, they kept alive some of the old customs, and the presence in the well would have been bloodily propitiated. How many were dragged screaming to their doom in that pit, the shrieks lost to the incessant beating of drums from the dark deeps of the forest...

"But at last, their dominion in this land ended, and a new race of men gradually spread across what had become the island of Britain. These fierce newcomers were tall and grim, and they were unequalled in warfare. They despised the conquered race and fell mercilessly upon them whenever they came across their settlements. The decayed, dwarf-like tribes of the forests could not stand against these new giants who carried weapons of bronze and worshipped strange gods. After many more years of increasing decline, the remnants of the old race only tarried on in the darkest combes of the wildwood or the deepest caves of the hills, woses and troglodyte creatures now of fairy tale and whispered rumour."

Wingood still stared at the old man as he spun his story. Large cumulus clouds were now gathering, and the sun was slowly obscured.

"As the aeons passed," Antrobus continued, "per'aps the fortunes of the Worm continued to decline. The new men, discovering its lair, would have shunned it. The well became hidden, lost in a dark tangle of forest, the primitive stones that guarded the old, cursed site, long tumbled and overgrown. The sacrifices and orgies of the old race became a myth in memory, the fires and weird drumming banished. And still the thing endured and, 'appen, it waited...

"Then, with the eventual coming of Christianity, a new fervour spread over the land and all signs of the heathen had to be hidden or erased. No longer simply a bogey of the forest, best avoided, the new faith could not countenance any continued 'devilish' presence at the Marchley Howe site. Clerics came seeking the Black Worm with book, bell and candle. Yet when they came to the Howe, the old, grassy mound that had, for long years covered the mouth of the pit, those early Christians failed to 'cleanse' it. Eventually, they must have found some means to 'contain' it and, it must have remained so for many centuries. But the presence was still felt. That's why I reckon the house has had more than its fair share of strange happenings since its foundation. Perhaps that's what drew Dashwood to seek out his old crony Venables. I don't know. But your Jerry or whoever he was working for... well, they must have decided that it was time something was done about it."

Wingood grunted and stood up brushing himself down carefully.

"What are you saying Jack? That the Devil himself will rise? It's all very Dennis Wheatley to me."

But Antrobus only smiled.

"The Devil himself? No, I don't think so. But perhaps *a* devil nevertheless... summat dark and old and utterly outlandish."

He turned to look at Wingood serious once more.

"Your Jerry is dead or gone... Nor can we contact whoever put him up to this..."

The old man sighed then, and a shadow seemed to pass over his face.

"But it seems," he added, almost in a whisper now, "to have fallen to us to do summat about it."

Antrobus looked up at the estate agent. Wingood thought he caught a queer gleam in the old man's eyes. Then, the westering sun burst through the gathering clouds. The meadow was transformed again, filled with a sudden light and warmth. But Wingood could smell rain in the air, and he shivered.

"Do you know Clive," Antrobus continued, "my family has been farming this land since records began. We spilt blood for it, cleared it, tamed it, and finally prospered on it. There's a mention of us in the Domesday Book as tenants under Earl Hugh of Deva. My lad runs the farm now, and one day it will be his. This place means something to me...."

Antrobus bent down and touched the ground at his feet and looked up at Wingood.

"Do you know, while I've a breath left in me, I'd rather be damned than stand by and let some dark thing... some 'Black Worm', whatever it is, creep into *my* county."

He stared at Wingood intently.

"Whether you like it or not, there are things in this world Clive... Strange things, things that science just can't explain..."

Wingood shook his head.

"I... that is, I just find it all very difficult to understand. You're talking about something that is really beyond my ken!"

Antrobus grunted.

"Oh aye?" he said sighing. "And therefore, dear Clive, as

a stranger give it welcome. There are more things in heaven and earth, Horatio, than are dreamt of in your philosophy."

Wingood blinked.

"Eh?"

But Antrobus straightened his shoulders and put his hand on Wingood's arm.

"Someone has to go back to Marchley Howe Clive, and, perhaps, complete whatever it was that the Jerry started. If I'm right about the date, then we know when it should be."

Wingood rolled his eyes.

"And then what should they do? Pour some holy water down the well, say a prayer?"

At first, Antrobus said nothing in reply. Instead, he loudly cleared his throat and spat. Then he turned back to stare at Wingood.

"Aye," he replied, smiling now, "summat like that."

With that he turned to face the gate that led back into the garden.

"Come on Clive, I've a nice old bottle of French Brandy in the cupboard."

And he strode away, leading the bemused Wingood back towards the farmhouse.

The two men were seated once more in Antrobus' sitting-room-come-study. The fire in the wood burner was now crackling merrily, its hearty light adding warm illumination to the rapidly darkening room. The deep rhythmic ticking of the hall clock marked the passing minutes. They both sat in thoughtful silence watching the dancing flames of the fire. Each cradled a brandy snifter, their glasses containing a generous measure of the golden liquor. Outside the day was quickly fading and the rain had finally arrived. It was now beating a steady tattoo on the panes of the narrow window.

Wingood turned to look at Antrobus. The old man was still looking at the fire, his craggy, hawk-nosed face weirdly illuminated by the flickering light of the fire itself and the soft, ambient glow of the nearby paraffin lamp.

Wingood took a deep draught of the brandy and then cleared his throat.

"Well Jack, I ought to get going, Doris will be wondering where I've gotten to..."

Antrobus nodded.

"Aye, I've got to feed the pigs and get the chickens in." He stood quickly and shook Wingood's hand.

"Very well, Clive. Just remember what I said. I need to take a peek myself in that cellar, and I'll go on my own if I must, but I'd rather have a bit of company... it would be wiser..."

Wingood inclined his head weakly and was suddenly glad of the warmth of the brandy inside of him. He stood up, curling his flat cap nervously in his hands.

"As I said Jack, I need to have a think about things. You must understand, it's all rather a lot to take in... but I will call you, I just need a day or so."

Antrobus snorted and drained his glass.

"Aye, alright," he said standing himself. He walked across to a cardboard box and rummaged inside.

"Here, take these. With my compliments."

Wingood stared at the pile of books in Antrobus' hands. He realised that they were copies of Antrobus' published works. Wingood recognised the cover of *Our mysterious County*, and beneath it was a copy of *Ghosts and Ghoulies of Our Country Lanes* and Antrobus' latest book, *Hellfire at Harvesttime*.

"Right," he said. "Er, thank you Jack, that's most kind."

Antrobus looked at Wingood keenly, as if deciding then and there whether he could rely on the other man or not.

"There's a lot to prepare if we decide to do this, so don't think about it for too long."

Nodding, and hefting up the books Antrobus had given him, Wingood said goodbye and left the farmhouse.

Wingood had had every intention of contacting Antrobus again the next day, at least once he had had time to think soberly about things, but the rainy Bank Holiday Monday had dragged slowly by and Wingood had, according to Doris, 'mooned about the house uselessly'. By Tuesday the drab mundanity of Wingood's life had reasserted itself and work had absorbed him once more into its routine. Three whole days had now passed before he reluctantly decided that it was time to call.

On Wednesday, Wingood waited until Debbie had left for the evening before he settled himself down at his desk and lifted the telephone receiver. Feeling suddenly anxious, he dialled Antrobus' number. The old man sounded surprised when he heard Wingood's voice on the telephone.

"Well, well, I wasn't sure if you'd get back in contact Clive. Are you ready to do this?"

There was a long pause. Wingood pushed his hand through his hair and sighed.

"Yes, I'm ready…"

He paused for a moment before continuing.

"The things you talked about… the incredible things… I don't understand it, but yes, I'm as ready as I ever will be I suppose."

He leaned back and closed his eyes.

"Good," Antrobus replied. "The first thing we need to do is go back to the house, a recce if you like."

Wingood looked puzzled.

"Recce?"

"Aye, a reconnaissance… a *recce*…" Antrobus replied.

Wingood sighed again.

"When?" he asked.

He heard Antrobus clear his throat.

"As soon as possible. How about this weekend?"

Wingood swallowed as he felt his heart rate suddenly increase.

"This weekend?" he said weakly. "Very well. What do I need to bring?"

There was a grunt at the other end of the line.

"Nowt. I have everything we'll need. Just wear sensible clothing, *dark* clothing. Leave your tie and brogues at 'ome."

Wingood nodded.

"Very well. Shall we say Saturday evening? I could be at your place for eight?"

Antrobus grunted once more.

"Aye, Saturday at eight then."

And with that he rang off.

Wingood was clearly distracted through the remaining days of that week. The weather remained dull and uninspiring, and the estate agency's business remained quiet. This meant that Wingood was largely confined to the office, working through a backlog of paperwork. But he was nervous and distracted, and uncharacteristically listless towards these administrative tasks. This was unusual enough for Debbie to take notice. She enjoyed her work at the estate agency, and in the three years that she had been working there, Debbie had become fond of her employer. Wingood was a considerate boss, and his strange shift of mood had really begun to unnerve her. But Debbie's numerous attempts to gently broach the topic were unsuccessful. Wingood only seemed to become more reserved and told her repeatedly that he was fine.

CHAPTER FOUR
THE RECCE

When Wingood arrived home that Saturday afternoon, he knew he had the house to himself for at least a couple of hours. Today, he remembered, Doris was having her hair 'done'. Kicking his shoes off, Wingood made himself a cup of tea and went to sit in the living room. For a few moments he sat in silence, staring blankly at the coffee table where he became mesmerised by the steam rising from the hot drink. Then, desperately trying to find a diversion, he got up and switched on the colour television set. The familiar strains of 'Abide with Me' reminded Wingood it was the day of the cup final. He sat back on the couch and stared at the television screen as the teams came out onto the pitch. Wingood lifted his tea and sipped it gingerly as the match commentator began.

"Well, here they come, into the sunshine... It's the moment

this 100,000 crowd has waited for. Ipswich on the right, in the blue tops. Arsenal in the red tracksuit tops..."

But Wingood was not listening. Although he continued to stare at the television screen, he no longer heard or saw. His thoughts had turned inwards, creeping back towards the looming shadow of that house. He was going back to Marchley Howe, tonight. And the nearer the time of the 'recce' came, the more nervous he felt. It was an anxious mix of fear coupled with a bloody-minded determination to keep his engagement with Antrobus. He felt his heart fluttering in his chest.

"Damn it!" he exploded, rising to his feet.

He switched the television off and went over to the sideboard to pour himself a whisky. His hand shook noticeably as he raised the glass to his lips. Closing his eyes, Wingood gulped the liquor down. Then he poured himself another one.

He closed his eyes once more and took several deep breaths, exhaling slowly.

"Better..." he muttered, belching.

But he could not settle.

Instead, Wingood went upstairs to his bedroom and pulled a briefcase from his wardrobe. Inside was his masonic regalia, apron and white gloves. Alongside these he now carefully packed a pair of black plimsolls, an old black jumper and a pair of dark slacks. His brown flat cap would have to do to complete the outfit. Closing the briefcase, he placed it on the bed and ran himself a bath.

When Doris eventually returned from town, Wingood

had made her a cup of tea, and once she was seated in the armchair with her slippers on, he had steeled himself and told her that he had had some unexpected news. Unfortunately, he had explained, he would have to drive up to Manchester for an extraordinary general meeting at the 'Lodge' tonight. It couldn't be helped, just one of those things.

"What? Again? You were only there last night!" she protested.

Wingood blushed.

"Yes Doris, it's just one of those things," he repeated. "I'm sure I won't be late..."

He watched her now, nervously awaiting a further reaction, but Doris kept her glare fixed on the television. Wingood had then retreated, apologising again as he closed the living room door.

He had left the house promptly at seven-thirty once he had finished washing the dinner dishes. When he was at last seated behind the wheel of the Jaguar he was overtaken by a sudden feeling of dark inevitability. His drive to Antrobus' farm passed all too quickly and he arrived at the white gate of Shippen Farm just before eight. Antrobus was waiting for him by the farmhouse door. He ushered Wingood inside and told him to change into his 'working gear'. Once Wingood was ready, Antrobus, grunting, hefted a large, olive-coloured canvas duffle bag, over his shoulder.

"What's in there?" Wingood asked looking at the bag quizzically.

"Stuff we'll need. You'll see."

Antrobus shut the old farmhouse door behind him.

"Any rate Clive," he now said with a wry smile, "let's be off and at it."

Wingood stared at the gates of Marchley Howe and gripped the steering wheel tightly. The closed metal barrier seemed starkly forbidding in the Jaguar's high beam headlights.

"Right," Antrobus murmured, climbing out of the passenger seat alongside him, "I'll just get these gates open."

Dumbly, Wingood nodded as Antrobus stepped quickly across to the unlocked gates. Glancing somewhat furtively about them, Wingood watched as the older man pushed the creaking metalwork open and stood aside for the car to enter. From his demeanour, Antrobus did not seem nervous at all, in fact, Wingood suspected that his co-conspirator was actually enjoying himself. Well, he mused darkly, *he* hasn't been in that house before. Shivering at the thought of what might await them, Wingood put the car back in gear and drove through the gates. After the gates were closed once more, Antrobus quickly climbed into the car.

"Let's be going before some farmer comes by and gets suspicious," he said.

Wingood remained quiet as they passed slowly through the woods. The reaching boughs of ancient trees arched over the car, weirdly illuminated by the passing beams of the Jaguar's headlights. He looked about apprehensively half-expecting a sudden rush from some ghastly figure.

At last, the car cleared the woods and the landscape opened up before them, but tonight was the new moon and the countryside, so bucolic and picturesque by daylight, was concealed in an inky blanket of darkness. To Wingood's nervous mind the land itself seemed possessed by an ominous and threatening wildness. Straining his eyes to stare across the estate, Wingood half-imagined he could already see the far shape of the house itself, a distant, looming mass, blacker than the dim park land that flanked it.

Sensing Wingood's rising nervous state, Antrobus patted his shoulder in an attempt at reassurance.

"Nowt to worry about Clive, we're just going to take a little look."

Wingood said nothing as he drove the car along the track towards the house. Once more he passed the entrance and made for the cobbled yard at the rear of the property. At last, he pulled on the handbrake and turned off the engine.

Antrobus switched on his torch.

"Ready?" he asked.

Wingood put his flat cap on and nodded.

"Let's get this over with," he said sighing.

Antrobus nodded, smiling grimly.

"Lay on, Macduff, And damn'd be him that first cries, 'Hold, enough!'"

And with that the two men climbed out of the car.

They entered the house through the forced window Wingood had employed the week before. Now they stood in the butler's pantry flashlights in hand. Antrobus placed a hand on Wingood's shoulder making the estate agent jump.

"Steady Clive," the older man said. "Now you lead the way."

They walked quietly, like burglars, and despite their remote location, the men were both strangely conscious not to make any unnecessary noise. Wingood, shining his torch before him, led Antrobus through the service areas to the front entrance hall. Here at last they paused and Antrobus looked about him cautiously.

"Oh aye," he breathed at last, seeming to take the measure of the place.

Antrobus shone his flashlight on the ground and unslung the duffle bag from his shoulder. This too he lay on the ground next to the flashlight.

"Right Clive," he said pointing at the arched door that led to the place below. "Down there is it?"

Wingood nodded mutely.

"Right," Antrobus repeated, spitting into his hands and rubbing them together. "All we are going to do is take a gander. No holy water today."

His smile returned and he patted Wingood on the back.

"Are you alright?"

Wingood turned to look at the old solid timber of the cellar door.

"Not really, but, as we are here, we may as well get on with it."

Antrobus nodded.

"Good... that's the spirit. As I say, we are only here to take a look."

He leaned down and picking up the flashlight, he opened the duffle bag and withdrew a small black case. He quickly pulled an object out of this case and Wingood saw it was a new 35mm SLR camera. Antrobus fitted a small flash attachment to the camera's hot shoe and cocked the shutter.

"Come on then. You carry the sack for me."

Picking up the duffle bag, Wingood followed Antrobus over to the timbered cellar door. Without hesitation, Antrobus turned the key in the ancient lock and pulled the door open.

Wingood winced despite himself as the door swung open revealing the dark aperture beyond. Leaning inside, Antrobus located the switch unit and flicked it on. The sudden illumination startled Wingood but as Antrobus quickly descended the time-worn stone steps, he found himself reluctantly following rather than be left alone in the echoing hallway. When he caught up with Antrobus the other man had paused at the base of the stairs and was staring around the ancient undercroft. Like Wingood had before him, he was looking about in amazement.

"Well, I'll be blowed," he said, evidently surprised at the brightness of the space. He looked at Wingood and winked.

"Just going to take a couple of shots... shouldn't need the flash in this light."

Setting the duffle bag down for a moment, Wingood rubbed his hands together, they were clammy and hot.

Seemingly satisfied with his photography, Antrobus nodded to Wingood.

"Come on Clive, lead the way."

Wingood started, then, swallowing, he picked up the duffle bag and began to walk towards the last chamber. There, he knew, lay the dark pit that was the entrance to the deep place below.

When they entered the last room, Antrobus walked without hesitation to the very lip of the well and seemed suddenly animated as he shone his torch down into the darkness. He whistled and then scratched his head wonderingly.

"Aye, oh aye, your Jerry was right..." he said turning to look at Wingood, his eyes shining. "'certain Andean ruins' he said, eh?"

Wingood nodded.

"Yes," was all he could manage in reply.

Antrobus took several photographs of the room and the opening of the pit. Then, he began to closely examine the broken fragments of timber and stone that lay piled neatly against the far wall. After some moments lifting and staring, he straightened up and nodded as if confirming some idea in his mind.

"Look here Clive, just look at this," he said pointing the camera excitedly at the blackened fragments of a beam.

Wingood placed the duffle bag down on the floor and walked over reluctantly, giving the edge of the pit as wide a berth as possible as he did so.

"What is it?" he asked hesitantly, squinting at the old

beam as Antrobus continued to take photographs from a variety of angles and distances.

"Look at these engravings in the wood," Antrobus suggested. "it's pitted and mouldy, but you can still make them out…"

But Wingood could see nothing that made any sense to him, and he shook his head.

"What is it?" he repeated bemused. "I can't see anything."

Antrobus slung the camera over his shoulder and ran his finger over a series of grooves in the rotting fragment.

"These are Enochian symbols Clive!" he hissed clearly excited by the discovery. "I'm bloody sure of it." He paused for a moment then, nodding said:

"Don't you see? These must have been put here by John Dee in the sixteenth century, *he* must have set up the seal that kept whatever was… or rather still *is*… down here, in place. The seal was broken by the Jerry, but maybe even these were no longer enough… they were certainly rotting."

Antrobus stroked his chin thoughtfully.

"Right then," he said, suddenly straightening up. "Like I said, time to take a gander."

Before Wingood could say anything, Antrobus returned to the duffle bag. He now pulled out a long coil of nylon rope and laid it carefully on the floor beside the rubble. Then he pulled out two hard hats fitted with lamps and portable battery packs. Wingood recognised them as miner's helmets.

"I got these from a mate of mine in Northwich, I was

writing summat about a haunting in a salt mine a couple of years ago, I just ended up keeping all the gear..."

Wingood looked at the helmets incredulously as Antrobus now took out two large walkie-talkies.

"You're not going down there are you!?" Wingood exclaimed, suddenly realising what Antrobus was doing. "I didn't think you were actually going down; I mean, we're just having a look, aren't we?"

But Antrobus did not answer at first. Instead, he began unravelling one end of the rope and started to make it fast to one of the nearby carved pillars that supported the arched roof high over their heads. Wingood watched flabbergasted as Antrobus pulled on the rope then, lifting up the thick coil, threw the remaining length of the rope down over the lip of the well.

"It's a recce Clive," Antrobus finally responded, turning back to Wingood, "I need to have a look and see what's down there... If we are going to... fix this, then I need to do this."

Wingood swallowed hard, trying to find the words.

"I didn't think you'd be actually... well, it's just mad! I'm not sure I even have the strength to lower you down..."

Antrobus shook his head.

"I'll be fine with this."

He pulled out something else from the duffle bag.

"This is a harness," he said as if that explained matters.

Wingood stared at the jumble of straps in Antrobus' hand and looked aghast.

"But really... go down? We don't know what's at the bottom or even how far down it is!"

Antrobus simply continued to fit the harness.

"Now then look, if we are to do this properly, we need to know the lie of the land. I must see the lair..."

Wingood stiffened.

"Lair!" he gasped. "You must be bloody crackers!"

Antrobus spat into the well and narrowed his eyes.

"Aye, well, mayhap I am, but I shouldn't be long. All you have to do is keep an eye on things up here. You can talk to me on this."

Antrobus handed Wingood one of the walkie-talkies.

"Tune it in to my channel there," he said pointing at the radio. "You press this button to speak and release it when you've said 'over'"

Ignoring Wingood's muttered protestations, Antrobus fitted the rope to the harness and pulled it through the loops of the support.

"You just keep your feet planted on the side and make sure nothing tangles or owt up here. Keep your miner's lamp lit in case the power goes again. The harness will hold me. It will be easy enough. If anything 'appens, I'll tell you on this," he said patting the walkie talkie that now hung around his neck.

Wingood stared at the harness and the rope once more.

"I'm not sure Jack, I mean... it's a bloody great hole in the floor! Can't we just lower a light down?"

But Antrobus shook his head emphatically.

"Nay, you're forgetting, there's a passage down there before the chamber. I have to see what's what."

Antrobus fitted the harness and adjusted his camera and walkie-talkie.

"All you have to do is stay calm, I'll do the rest." He looked at Wingood reassuringly.

Wingood stared back doubtfully.

"I never... Are you...? I mean, can you...?"

Antrobus laughed now guessing Wingood's thoughts.

"I'm stronger than I look. Trust me, it'll be fine. Just keep an eye on things for me."

Before Wingood could raise any further objections, Antrobus pointed to the side of the pit.

"Stand here," he instructed.

Wingood stared, his heart suddenly pounding. This was not what he had imagined at all. But if Antrobus was worried he wasn't showing any signs of it. Before Wingood could protest further, the older man took hold of the rope and gave it a firm tug. Then, seemingly satisfied and nodding to the horrified Wingood, he stood with his back to the hole.

"Right, here I go."

Leaning backwards with a grunt, he began to edge over the lip of the well, using the great smooth rocks of the wall as vertical steppingstones as he now slowly began to lower himself down.

"Watch that rope now, see it doesn't rub too much on the edge," he reminded his companion.

Wringing his hands, Wingood watched as Antrobus

began his descent. His eyes followed the old man's light as it danced across the huge boulders of the well's wall. The other man swiftly dropped lower and lower, bouncing down the wall as he went. Wingood continued to stare as the light of his new friend's helmet became ever smaller and smaller.

"By 'eck!" he heard Antrobus' faint shout as the man continued to descend. "It's getting colder... but these walls are fantastic! I'm glad I brought my camera! Oh, the bloody cold..."

Wingood shuddered.

"Shhh," he muttered nervously, half to himself.

But Antrobus continued to exclaim excitedly as, yard by yard, he swiftly slipped further into the depths. Once, Wingood saw Antrobus, now a distant, shrinking figure, starkly illuminated by the light of the camera's flash.

The descent did not take as long as Wingood had thought it might. The rope became suddenly slack and was followed by a distant, crackling shout over the walkie talkie.

"Right! I'm at the bottom! Over!"

Antrobus' voice seemed breathless mixed with the sound of rising static.

Wingood could still see the vague light of Antrobus' helmet, but now it looked like a dim and faraway star.

"There's a passage alright," the old man continued. "but it doesn't look natural. It's huge! I'm going in, hold on! Over!"

Then the light disappeared and Wingood could only hear the static.

"Jack?" he called. He pressed the button on the walkie talkie and twisted the tuner. "Jack!?"

His desperate voice echoed into the depths but there was now no answering voice from the radio. Wingood saw that that the rope remained slack. Once again, he found himself standing, staring into the pit, occasionally casting nervous glances around the brightly illuminated chamber. Uncomfortably, he remembered the strange noises and sounds he had heard on his last visit, and he shuddered involuntarily. Hand shaking slightly, he reached into his jacket pocket and found the cigarettes he had bought at the garage. He lit one and began to smoke as he turned his attention back to the radio set.

"Jack? Hello, Jack Antrobus?" he hissed into the mouthpiece of the walkie-talkie. "Are you there, Jack... Over!"

His voice was a harsh, distressed whisper, but it faded into nothingness.

Minutes passed as hours. Wingood shifted his weight from one foot to the other nervously, chain-smoking, listening in vain for any sound from the walkie-talkie. His mind raced as he wondered what was happening down there. It seemed to be taking too long. Surely Antrobus had seen enough?

Just as he was about to call out again, he thought he caught a flash of distant light in the dizzying depths below. With sweating hands, he now fumbled to speak into the radio.

"Jack? Hello? Jack!"

The rope suddenly became taught and then the walkie-talkie crackled back into life.

"I'm coming up! Over."

Sighing in relief, Wingood watched as his companion's light now shone upward. Antrobus hoisted himself up gradually, jerkily rising, yard by slow yard.

At last, Wingood was able to reach down and pull at Antrobus as he neared the top edge of the well.

The old man scrambled up and sitting on the edge of the pit, tried to catch his breath and began rubbing his cold arms. His legs still dangled over the black maw of the well. He looked at Wingood wearily and then nodded.

"Aye, well. Come on, help me up."

Wingood stepped cautiously forward to the edge of the well and helped Antrobus carefully to his feet. The older man slowly disentangled himself from his harness.

"Well, what did you see?" Wingood asked breathlessly.

Antrobus looked at him.

"It's just bloody fantastic... But," he muttered, "I think we're going to need dynamite,"

Wingood started.

"Dynamite? Why? What on earth... Where the hell are we going to get that!?"

Without answering, Antrobus hauled the rope out of the well and coiled it neatly on the floor.

"Let's get going and then we can talk," was all he said at last.

Only too relieved that the 'recce' was finally over,

Wingood nodded eagerly and began to remove his miner's helmet.

Antrobus bent down and retrieved Wingood's cigarette ends from the floor. He slipped them into his jacket pocket.

"Best not leave any sign we've been here, you never know," Antrobus warned, tapping the side of his nose.

He turned to untie the rope and, coiling the remainder, he proceeded to re-pack the duffle bag with all the equipment. Putting out the light of his own helmet, he pushed it into the bag as well, then tightened the draw string.

"Come on then Clive, let's go home," he said, mopping his brow.

On the car journey back to Shippen Farm, Antrobus had told Wingood all about his descent into the pit and how his initial suspicions, about the age and the nature of the situation, had only been confirmed by what he had seen. Wingood tried to listen, to absorb what the older man was saying, but everything he heard made him feel both more anxious and filled with an ever-increasing dread. Antrobus on the other hand seemed filled with a barely suppressed, fay excitement.

"It's so old Clive, just as I had imagined it, but even more... *impressive*... if that's the right word. You've seen the pit? Well, the passage is twice the size of it, round and smooth like some great tube, paved all about with those cunningly fitted boulders. I tell you, each one of them must weigh a couple of tons. And the cold! You'd think there was a refrigeration unit running down there! I've been in plenty of caves and potholes, but I've never seen owt... *felt* owt, like it. We're going to need warmer clothes..."

The road was quiet as they wound back along dark country lanes. Wingood now had a growing headache.

"What was this chamber like then? The one at the end of the passage?" he managed to ask at last.

"Worst of all," Antrobus replied grimly. "It's big, but I didn't go in far. You can feel... summat." He remained quiet for a moment before continuing. "The cave might be natural, but I doubt it. The walls and floor are seamless, completely smooth and it's black," he shook his head. "I don't mean dark, I mean it's like black glass, but it seemed to just *soak up* the torchlight..."

Wingood felt more uncomfortable as Antrobus tried to convey what he had felt.

"Aye, there's summat down there, but I saw nowt, just felt... well felt... a sort of *nothingness*..." he scratched his nose thoughtfully for a moment. "What I mean is, it felt like a *negation*... a void..." "."

Wingood glanced across at his passenger.

"What was all that about dynamite then?" he asked his voice cracking slightly.

Antrobus shrugged.

"Luck is where opportunity meets preparation, a Roman once said. We just might need it, that's all."

Wingood shivered and glanced across once more.

"Jack... Next time... Will I have to go down there with you...? I mean down the hole...?"

Antrobus grunted.

"Aye, I reckon I'll need your help."

He turned to look at Wingood almost pityingly. Wingood was now staring ahead, gripping the steering wheel tightly.

"I'm going to do a bit of digging," Antrobus submitted at last. "I know someone who might be able to shed a bit of light on things, at least once I've shown him those photographs that I've taken. It'll take me a few days, but it might help us decide on how best to proceed."

Wingood dropped Antrobus at the gate of Shippen Farm, and the two men shook hands and said their farewells. Antrobus told Wingood that he would be developing the camera's film immediately and he promised to call Wingood as soon as he had any news.

As he turned for home, Wingood's headache steadily worsened.

"Hello Clive," Antrobus' crackling voice said on the other end of the line. "Are you ready to have a chat?"

Wingood had been dreading Antrobus' call, but he had also paradoxically been willing the days to pass. In the end he had been, despite his own inner turmoil, eager to hear from the writer again. But several days had passed and Antrobus had not called. Growing concerned, Wingood had tried phoning Shippen Farm several times. Yet, alarmingly to Wingood, whatever time of the day or evening he called, the phone had just rung and rung. Antrobus was either not home or could not answer. Wingood had been planning to drive out there when he had a chance to find out if Antrobus was alright.

Now he held the telephone receiver tightly against his ear.

"Where have you been?" he whispered urgently.

"Never mind that," Antrobus snapped back grumpily. "Just meet me at the Atheling's Arms in Netherton... tomorrow. That's handy for you and the landlord has some good ale. I'll tell you all my news then. Say one o'clock?"

Wingood agreed and hung up. He glanced now habitually at the calendar on the office wall. Forty-one days until the twenty-first, the night of the solstice. His nerves, he had decided, could not take much more of this waiting and Debbie would keep insisting on asking if he was 'alright'. No, the sooner things ended, well, the better, he thought. Then life could return to some normality, or at least so he hoped.

Wingood knew the Atheling's Arms well, it wasn't quite his local, but it was familiar enough. The next day, he strolled down the high street from the office and made for the old coaching inn. The bar was fairly busy with its usual assortment of Friday lunchtime drinkers; farmers, in for a quick half, a couple of thirsty lorry drivers and a range of other locals all enjoying a drink. Wingood went over to the bar looking about for Antrobus.

"What will it be sir, oh Mr. Wingood isn't it?"

Wingood smiled and nodded at the barman.

"Hello Bill, a pint of best bitter please."

The bearded barman began to pull his pint as Wingood looked around once more. He spotted Antrobus now, the old man was seated in the corner of the inglenook, his head wreathed in pipe smoke, his keen eyes peering at Wingood from the dark corner. Antrobus raised his glass in greeting.

"Best pour me another one, please Bill," Wingood said turning back to the barman. "My friend's glass looks nearly empty."

Wingood carried the two pints of beer over to the inglenook and seated himself next to Antrobus. It was a warm day outside and he was glad that the fire remained unlit.

"Ow do Clive," Antrobus said raising his glass once more. "Your good health."

Wingood stared at him.

"Where the heck have you been?" he began earnestly. "I've tried calling several times…"

Antrobus raised a gnarled hand.

"All right Clive, All right… I've been away you see? I had a little trip down south, to London in fact."

Wingood's eyes widened.

"London!" he exclaimed loudly.

He suddenly looked about him self-consciously.

"London?" he repeated, now lowering his voice.

Antrobus smiled and nodded.

"Aye, bloody London," he answered. "I had to see a man about those pictures. I 'ave a contact at the British Museum, another Jerry as it 'appens, or an Austrian at least… so I called him up and told him I had something to show him. I didn't want to post them; I didn't want them getting lost and wasting any time. So, when he reluctantly agreed to meet with me, I packed a bag and off I went."

As if that explained everything, Antrobus picked up his new pint and drank deeply. Then, smacking his lips, he wiped his hand across his mouth, seemingly satisfied.

"Aye, like I said, good ale... an increasingly rare thing in these benighted times."

Wingood sat back and sighed.

"What did this 'contact' tell you then?" he asked, now sipping at his own beer.

Antrobus frowned.

"Well, it wasn't a wasted journey. This fella I know, let's call him Manfred, he looks down his nose at me a bit. After all, he has a 'reputation' to uphold at the museum, and in his eyes I'm just some sensationalist hack who makes a living from writing about folklore, superstitions and other dubious 'nonsense'." Antrobus grinned broadly. "But that's all right, you see, I'd helped him out once, quite a long time ago, just after the war, when I was still in the military police. Anyhow, now I was calling in the favour and the slate could be wiped clean. But even I had never imagined that our little 'adventure' would have such an impact on him.

"We agreed to meet at a nearby hotel, in one of them fancy wine bars they 'ave down there, he certainly didn't want me anywhere near his office in the museum. At any rate, he soon changed his tune when he saw those photographs."

Antrobus became suddenly serious once more and

tapping out his pipe in the ash tray, he looked at Wingood intently.

"Manfred spent a long time staring at the photographs. Occasionally he would glance up at me quizzically. But I didn't say owt, I just let him study them pictures."

Wingood coughed.

"Yes, but what did he say?"

"Well, first off, he demanded to know when and where they had been taken. I told him I wasn't able to say exactly, but I did say that I had taken them only a few days before, here in England. That fact seemed to shake him... I told him I wanted confirmation about the possible age of the structures.

"Turning his eyes back to the photographs, Manfred took his time going through them, looking over each black and white print again and again. But I left him to it. At length, he turned back to me. His face was now gleaming with perspiration, oh aye, it was a warm day, but it was cool in the bar... and he was sweating. Anyhow, he just looks at me for a minute then he says, 'I have seen this type of structure before but not here, not in Europe' he went all quiet for a moment, but I held off saying owt and just waited for him to continue. 'Well,' he says at last. 'I saw something like this in Bolivia years ago... forty years ago in fact, deep underground...' Now he had this faraway look in his eyes as he spoke, like he was talking to himself. 'Yes,' he continued. 'It's just the same, but it *can't* be...' He slapped his hand down on the table and looked hard at me. Then, leaning over the table, he hissed; 'Did you find anything... hear... anything *else* down there?'.

"Of course, I asked him what he meant though I thought I could guess it. He just looked at me through narrowed eyes for a minute, then he said: 'I think that you have. And I urge you not to return to... wherever this is... you don't know what you are dealing with.' At that point I says to him that was exactly why I was talking to *'im*, and I needed to know. Without answering, he called the waiter over and settled our bill.

"Then he invited me to walk with him for a bit. I agreed, intrigued now, and in short order we ended up sitting on a park bench in Russell Square. Like I said, it was a hot day, and the shade of the trees was a pleasant refuge from the growing heat of the afternoon. I just sat there, my eyes following the unending traffic and the busy, rushing crowds - wondering why anyone would choose to live in a place like this - when he began to talk. He told me how, when he was still a student in Germany, he had been 'given the honour', along with several of the other top students in his cohort, of being invited to assist his young professor, one Dr. Hermann Kruger, on an archaeological fieldtrip to Bolivia... That had been in late 1938. In an introductory lecture illustrated by glowing lantern slides, Kruger demonstrated to his selected scholars how he had identified the proposed site of the dig using aerial photographs. Something about the layout of the area suggested fabulous and intriguing archaeological possibilities. Now, he could reveal that, with support from

Himmler himself, the finances were finally in place to begin."

Antrobus paused to drink.

"Well?" Wingood asked, his mind now perplexed with wonder at the turn of the conversation.

"Well," Antrobus said, "I could tell now that Manfred had a memory of something that he was desperate to share, something in those photographs had jolted him. His patronising manner had all but evaporated and he seemed eager now to tell his story to a willing ear. So, I listened.

"It seems that although they had been given all the latest equipment and were well financed by both the university *and* the German government, the official expedition was spectacularly unsuccessful. Once they had trekked into the Andes to the proposed site, it hadn't taken them long to make several discoveries in the first few weeks of the dig, Kruger had evidently been correct in identifying the site as an ancient settlement, but their conscientious and methodical excavation revealed nothing epoch-making. They unearthed a dozen skulls and corresponding bone fragments in what had evidently been a reliquary, many ceramic shards of the crudest kind were unearthed as well as some rough beads and a few remnants of piled stonework that suggested a building. As a result, a general feeling of gloom had descended over the initially enthusiastic young students whose hopes and toil now seemed to be in vain. By the end of the month, they had barely had enough artifacts to fill more than two small and carefully packed wooden crates. Far from being the greatest archaeological discovery since Schliemann's Troy or Carter's Tutankhamun, Kruger's expedition was turning out to be something of a damp squib.

However, for the rest of the men, the most unsettling thing of all was the behaviour of the expedition's leader. For Kruger seemed oddly unperturbed by the paucity of the dig's findings. Instead, he began to ride out alone, always driving his stout pony upwards, towards the lowering mist encircled peaks. The students would pause from their work to watch as Kruger climbed higher and higher until, at last, he would disappear from view as he entered the dense forests that crowned the precipitous upper reaches. After several days absence Kruger would return, but he remained aloof and, beyond the simplest courtesies, he did not share his thoughts with any of his comrades. When Kruger returned to camp after his third sojourn into the upper forests, he was no longer alone. Following behind the archaeologist's pony was an old, strangely tattooed Quechua medicine man.

"For a few days Kruger had shut himself away, working alone in his tent, attended only by the Indian. Then Kruger finally took some into his confidence. Seven of the burliest, most athletic and brightest of the student lads (one of whom of course was Manfred) were at last summoned to a meeting in Kruger's tent. When the puzzled youngsters arrived, they saw that a man called Bauer, one of the more experienced pre-historians was also there, as was a sour-looking geologist named Hahn. In addition, there was one other member of the larger expedition team who had been invited to the meeting. This was a quiet, reserved character, whose position had remained something of a mystery to all of them save Kruger himself, but whom the others suspected must be 'Himmler's agent'. This man had always remained aloof from the other members of the expedition throughout their time in Bolivia, and most tellingly of all, he had shown no more than a cursory interest in the progress of the dig.

When they were all either seated on the ground or perched on sagging camp chairs, Kruger began. He told them that they had been selected for what he called a mission of 'supreme, national importance'. The site of the 'official' dig had merely been a ruse, a cover for the real task in hand. The dig would now proceed in what he called 'camp alpha', high in the cloud forest. He had, he further informed them, at last a chance to prove Edmund Kiss correct, that a diaspora of Nordic Thulians had indeed settled the new world ages before. The men listened with wonder as Kruger told them that he had discovered something on those lonely excursions, high up into the dense forests above them. But in answer to the excited questions of the group, he would reveal nothing about this special 'find'. Instead, he urged only obedience and patience. Whatever this find was, it had clearly convinced the archaeologist that his theories were correct. This object had been carefully packed by Kruger himself, and sent, with all haste, directly to Prinz-Albrecht-Strasse in Berlin, where Himmler had awaited its arrival.

With evident triumph, Kruger now pulled a folded piece

of paper from his jacket pocket and read it to us aloud. It was a telegram from Himmler himself.

*Dr Kruger. Artefact received. A *most* important discovery. Proceed with all speed to secure the site. Procure any necessary resources through usual channels. Codeword Breakthrough. Awaiting a successful outcome and detailed report. Heil Hitler. H.H.*

They were not told what 'Codeword Breakthrough' signified. Instead, they were sworn to secrecy, and within a week all the preparations had been made. Despite their bewilderment, most of the young men were excited by the intriguing turn of events and hope of an archaeological triumph was rekindled. On the day of their departure, they rose early and, as the eastern sky slowly lightened, they were each issued with climbing and caving gear. The party silently departed the main camp before the first light of dawn and began an arduous hike, high into the surrounding mountainous forests.

"Their guide was the same, silent Indian who now led them higher and higher along winding paths, until they came, at last, to the dense forests above. They laboured on, scrambling and climbing after the seemingly inexhaustible Indian. Finally, after several hours' hard ascent, the guide suddenly halted. Before them loomed the yawning entrance of a great chasm, stark and black against the frame of the verdant forest. Manfred said that it was immediately both a fantastic and unsettling place. The opening in the rock was surrounded by gargantuan, twisted trees and vines, crowned by dense, spectral mists that drifted weirdly through the canopy. Looking about him then and suddenly showing marked signs of nervousness, the Quechua man sniffed the air and declared that he would go no further. After demanding his payment, he quickly turned and abandoned them. Untroubled by the loss of their guide, Kruger allowed the team only a short time to recover from their long, gruelling ascent. All too soon Kruger gave the order for the team to prepare their caving equipment. Once everybody was kitted out, the eager archaeologist led the foray into the darkness before them.

"At first the caverns of the initial descent were wide, high and fairly level, but the deeper they went; the more difficult conditions would soon become. Before very long, they were rappelling down yawning sinkholes and crawling through flooded and cramped, claustrophobic tunnels. All the while, Kruger tirelessly led the way, his eyes wide with an almost manic determination. And then, at last, they *did* find something. Protruding from the sand of one of the many winding tunnels they came across an ancient, human skull. It was quickly examined, and a strange light had grown in Kruger's eyes. As he slowly removed the callipers from the cracked and toothless remains, he said with a breathless whisper, '*Nordic...*'. With a nod from the archaeologist, the relic was fully unearthed and packed carefully away.

"Seemingly convinced that he was indeed on the right track, Kruger pushed the party on at what Manfred said was a dangerous, reckless pace. Finally, after abseiling down yet another, steep-sided pit, they suddenly emerged through the roof of a massive, arena-like space. As they descended excitedly on their ropes, their dancing lanterns fell across a gigantic, ruinous monolith that now reached up from below them. The team, silenced into awe, unslung their ropes and slowly followed their leader as he crossed the wide, open space in order to better examine the monolith. On the few parts of the monument that remained somewhat intact, they could make out the time-worn remains of huge, bas-relief figures. Some of these carvings clearly depicted an advanced form of humanity. Tall, Homeric figures stood fully armoured. On seeing these Kruger had murmured to the group excitedly, 'Here is a relic of the ancient Aryans!'.

"But there were other forms depicted as well, disquieting, anthropomorphic beast-men, and these creatures seemed to be at war with the humans. Manfred remembers one particularly disturbing and most alien representation. Though the wall here was badly degraded, Manfred could still make out something roughly anthropoid in the time-blasted form, but it had claws like sabres and its head seemed to converge in a mass of writhing tentacles. Hanging, bat-like wings completed the nightmarish depiction…

"Kruger *still* did not pause. Manfred and some of the others had wondered at this. But Kruger had his goal in sight. For just beyond the cracked and leaning pillar gaped the entrance to a high, round tunnel. According to Manfred, this tunnel was the mirror image of the one in my photographs…

"Kruger was now ecstatic as if he had been *expecting* to find this entrance. He ordered a meticulous examination of the monolith and the surrounding cavern floor; everything was to be documented and photographed exhaustively. But the archaeologist was even more eager to continue and, leaving the bulk of the party in that cyclopean gallery, he selected one man to accompany him as he determined to press on further into the great tunnel itself. This choice of companion was the mysterious individual whose role neither Manfred, nor any of the other members of the party, were privy to. It was now quietly assumed that the man must indeed be a representative of the *Reichsführer* himself. Whatever the case, it was evident from the fact that Kruger had chosen him to accompany him on the next phase of his exploration, that the man must be of some importance.

"Kruger and the other man soon left the main party and disappeared into the vast mouth of the tunnel. The others watched as their lights slowly dwindled away. Neither man was ever seen alive again."

Antrobus drained his glass.

"My round Clive?"

Wingood, absorbed by the tale now started out of his reverie.

"Eh? Oh yes," he glanced at his watch. "Just one more, then I'll have to be off."

Nodding, Antrobus walked over to the bar and ordered their drinks.

Wingood looked about him trying to re-anchor himself with the plain reality of the surroundings of the cosy inn. But he could barely suppress a shiver when Antrobus returned from the bar with their beer.

THE HORROR BENEATH

"Cheers..." he mumbled. "So, what happened then?" he said raising his glass.

Antrobus looked at him quizzically.

"Eh? What happened when?"

Wingood coughed on his beer.

"The expedition," he spluttered. "What happened to them?"

Antrobus nodded and began to re-fill his pipe.

"Aye, well," he said, lighting a match and putting it to the tobacco. "They sent a group down the tunnel after an hour or two when Kruger and that other fella didn't return. The remaining group were only too conscious of how far and how deep they had travelled, the older men were already near exhaustion, and, at any rate, they would soon need more oil for their lanterns nor would the batteries in their electric lamps last forever. In addition, their tents and food supplies were still with the stores and equipment left near to the entrance of the caves. Most worrying of all Manfred said, there was a creeping feeling of disquiet amongst them. The initial excitement at their clearly historic discovery had soon, surprisingly, ebbed away. The men went about their tasks in a muted, even nervous manner. It seemed that the longer they remained in that wide, cheerless pit, the greater their anxiety became.

"Manfred was one of the four men who volunteered for the 'rescue' mission to find Kruger. Leaving the others, the group of them pressed on, following in Kruger's footsteps. There were no other exits from the monstrous passage, and besides, they could clearly see the tracks of the two men, their boot prints visible in the disturbed layers of sand and dust on the tunnel's floor.

"After walking for some time, they found Kruger and his companion at last. Their bodies, or what remained of them, were lying on the floor at the entrance to a huge cavern or grotto. Stepping fearfully into the massive open space, they began to examine the corpses and were disturbed to discover that both men seemed, dried out, *mummified*, as if all life and substance had simply been drained away. As disturbing as this discovery was, they were even more distressed by the situation of the bodies.

"The quiet stranger, the man they had supposed must be a Gestapo agent, was dressed in a robe, like a monk's habit but made of a dark silk and covered in carefully stitched runic symbols. There were more runes drawn in the sand of the floor and the remnants of a circle of guttering candle stumps. Cast aside, in the dust and dirt next to Kruger's now horribly shrivelled body, lay an old volume. Manfred had been the first to notice the large book. With trembling hands, he had picked it up and carefully shaken the dust from the heavy tome. The book was bound with a cracked and worm-eaten black leather that was held in iron facings. But despite its evident age, Manfred could still make out the outline of the time-worn, hand-engraved title: *De Vermis Mysteriis*. That translates as something like, *The Mysteries of the Worm*..." Antrobus explained before continuing.

"Opening it, he saw that the old, yellowed pages, were printed in a heavy, Blackletter text, but he had no difficulty in recognising and reading the language. It was Latin. The short fragment that he had read was enough to convince him that he was in the presence of something wholly... unnatural... *aberrant*. Confounded and still dazed, he had, with great care, placed the large book into his rucksack. Then the group, utterly confused and disturbed by their grim discovery, now made a unanimous and hasty retreat. Filled with revulsion and mystified by their find, they still had enough composure between them to carry the remains of their two dead comrades away from the frightful scene. However, this did not require any great effort on the part of the four young men, as both bodies were entirely desiccated.

"Carrying their grim burdens between them, they quickly made their way back without incident. But, when they arrived at the end of the tunnel, they were appalled to discover that the remainder of their companions had seemingly vanished. The dozen or so lanterns that had been fixed to the wall of the cave, still burned wanly, but all the rest of the equipment lay scattered across the floor in a chaos of disorder. At first, they thought that the others had simply abandoned them, and they spent several minutes running to and fro, calling and shouting in desperation. But when they finally examined the scene more closely, they had been disturbed to discover that none of the expedition's equipment was missing. Lamps, ropes, harnesses, even rucksacks filled with personal items, all remained accounted for. If indeed the men had fled, then why had they done so blindly, not even taking a lamp between them? When the four remaining men began to dazedly gather the scattered items together, they quickly discovered that some of the equipment had been crushed flat as if compressed by some unknown, great weight. More unsettling were the many inexplicable, wide smooth tracks newly impressed across the ancient dust of the cavern floor. But there was no other sign of the rest of the party whatsoever. As panic now threatened to overwhelm them, the four men were further dismayed to hear an uncanny sound echoing up from the prodigious tunnel behind them.

"Manfred said that he never identified the source of the noise, but he was convinced that it was not... *natural*. There was no wind down there, no draught or current of air. He said it sounded like a ghastly, musical piping sound."

Wingood had the sudden shiver of someone walking over his grave. Trembling slightly, he placed his beer down on the table next to him.

"And then?" he asked, his voice now almost a whisper.

"Aye, well," Antrobus answered. "They grabbed what they needed, left the bodies of the two men where they lay, and climbed out of there as fast as they could."

He supped at his pint and looked at Wingood.

"Manfred said that the return journey was the worst thing of all. Two of them got out, just about. They lost one man along the way when he became entangled in his climbing harness on one of their steep ascents. Abandoning him in their terror of what followed, they were haunted by the trapped man's desperate screams, screams that were soon abruptly cut off... After that, one fella just threw his arms in the air and fled from his companions, screaming for his mother. Exhausted and terrified, the two remaining men desperately climbed, crawled and scrambled their way through the darkness, all the while their lights dimming... And always, just on the edge of hearing, was that sound, pursuing them... A musical, piping whine that Manfred said still haunts his dreams, a sound that, he swears, he will never forget..."

He paused and looked at Wingood.

"Well, they made it back to the camp. On the way they agreed to say nothing of what they had seen, and they concocted a story of a cave-in that had killed the rest of the party somewhere deep in the caverns...

"After that, they returned to Germany and the expedition was seemingly forgotten as the dark years of the war began...

"But Manfred had summat he wanted me to have, was glad to give me in fact..."

Now turning, Antrobus carefully lifted a large bulky object from the bench beside him, it was tightly wrapped in a red silk cloth.

"And... here it is."

He placed the bundle on the table next to his pint and then slowly removed the cloth.

Wingood stared fearfully at the worn, black leather cover of the old book.

Antrobus drained his glass quickly.

"So now I have to go up to York."

Wingood, dragged his eyes away from the tome on the table to gape at the old man.

"York? What on earth for?" he asked apprehensively.

Antrobus carefully wrapped the book back in its cloth.

"I have to know more about this book, see? There's an antiquarian bookshop in York that specialises in this sort of thing. If this book can help us, then we need to know how."

Wingood looked at the man doubtfully.

"It didn't seem to do that... what was his name? Kruger... any good, did it?"

Antrobus snorted.

"Aye, well, at any rate, maybe I can find out what they *thought* that they were doing."

He looked at Wingood intently.

"Don't you see Clive? We need to have as much information as possible before we try and fix this? If knowing about this... this 'Mysteries of the Worm', gives us half a chance of working it out, well, then it's worth it in my book!"

Wingood sighed and finished his pint glumly.

"Alright Jack, I suppose you are right. But keep in touch, will you? Phone me at some point and keep me updated..." he paused, then asked, "When are you going?"

Antrobus nodded.

"Right away," he said. "I'm all packed."

Wingood glanced at where Antrobus was pointing and saw the familiar, bulky shape of his duffle bag lying on the floor at the man's feet.

"I'll be in York by seven tonight," the writer explained.

Wingood blinked.

"I see..."

The estate agent stood now, preparing to leave.

Antrobus reached out and held his arm.

"There is one more thing I need to tell you."

Wingood looked at him expectantly.

"Yes? What is it, Jack?"

Antrobus cleared his throat, and he pulled the stem of his pipe from his mouth.

"Manfred told me the name of that other fella who died alongside Kruger," Antrobus explained. "It was a name he had not thought about for forty years... until that is, he read it again recently in the press."

Wingood looked at him, now puzzled.

"Eh? What name?"

Antrobus frowned darkly.

"Von Hallerstein," he muttered. "Kruger's mysterious companion was called von Hallerstein..."

Wingood's face blanched and he collapsed back down onto his seat.

"Von Hallerstein!" he exclaimed. "How!... I mean it must just be a coincidence"

Antrobus snorted again.

"Don't be bloody daft Clive," he said sharply. "Coincidence? No! Whoever this man was he must have been connected to *our* von Hallerstein. That's an unusual aristocratic name. No, Clive, it's not a bloody coincidence."

Wingood shook his head as the two men sat in silence for some moments, the laughter and chatter of conversation all about them, still seeming distant and strange.

At last, his mind still reeling from Antrobus' revelations, Wingood rose to his feet once more.

"I have to go... Look, just please, keep in touch."

Antrobus nodded, shaking Wingood's proffered hand warmly.

"Oh, and Jack," Wingood added as he turned to leave. "Good luck."

Wingood waited for the expected call all weekend, but he did not hear anything further from Antrobus until Tuesday evening.

"Hello Clive, just calling as promised," Antrobus voice seemed far away and there was a slight echo on the line.

"What have you found out?" Wingood ventured somewhat nervously.

There was a pause and then Wingood heard Antrobus speaking to someone else.

"Hang on Clive... Yes, thank you love... Sorry Clive, just getting a cup of tea... Right, where was I?"

Wingood took a deep breath.

"Have you found anything out about the book?"

The line crackled and Wingood heard the ceramic clink of a cup being set on a saucer.

"Aye, I have as a matter of fact," Antrobus answered. "Dennis de Clerc, the book seller, is very excited by the book; once I had convinced him of the provenance - I gave him the *abridged* version of Manfred's tale - his first impulse was to offer me a lot of money for it..." Antrobus chuckled. "I told him no, but that if I was able to use the book, to understand the contents, well then, he could have it as a gift... at least once I was finished with it. I don't know what he thinks I'm up to but the chance of owning the bloody thing has convinced him to help," Antrobus paused before continuing. "Actually, that's unfair, he would have helped me anyway, he's a good lad and as keen as anything. At any rate, we've set to work going through it, I'm at his place now having a cup of tea with his mother in the kitchen... Dennis reckons it will take us at least a week or two of evening work to get a rough outline of the contents. My Latin is not that good, but Dennis reads it like a Roman."

Wingood took a sharp intake of breath.

"A fortnight!" he exclaimed. "Are you sure this is necessary?"

He heard Antrobus' sigh on the other end of the line.

"I only wish it weren't Clive," he retorted. "Even the little we've translated so far gives me ruddy gooseflesh..."

Now Antrobus lowered his voice as if suddenly wishing not to be overheard.

"Look, we still have some time and I have a growing feeling that this book can help us stop whatever is happening under Marchley Howe. If it can, in anyway help us, then it's got to be worth the effort."

Wingood sighed.

"Alright Jack, thanks for calling and keep me updated, will you?"

He heard Antrobus slurp at his tea.

"Aye, I will Clive... Oh, and Clive?"

"Yes?" Wingood answered.

"Just try to relax a little, try to act normal. Once I've

worked this out, I'll be straight back 'ome and then we can decide on our best course of action..."

Wingood sighed deeply as he replaced the receiver.

In the end, Antrobus was away for more than a fortnight. Wingood tried to immerse himself in work matters but although things in the office were running smoothly, largely due to Debbie's relentless proficiency, and business was indeed once again picking up, Wingood felt like a bad actor in a cheap play. Still, he reassured himself, he was keeping up appearances, and he was sure nobody suspected the fear and inner turmoil that now habitually consumed him. But the deceit and the waiting continued to take its toll on him, and he was more than relieved when Antrobus finally travelled home from York towards the end of the third week since their last meeting in the Atheling's Arms. At the time of Antrobus' return, it was only twenty-seven days until the solstice.

Wingood and Antrobus arranged to meet again at Shippen Farm the following Sunday. Wingood arrived mid-afternoon, and, as usual, Antrobus was waiting for him when he pulled up in his Jaguar.

"Now then, Clive," the writer said welcoming him warmly. "Come on through."

Wingood followed Antrobus through the low doorway of the farmhouse. They walked through the dark, cool interior and Wingood was led back out through the back door in the kitchen, then through the ever-burgeoning vegetable garden, and finally, out into the back meadow. Wingood saw two cane chairs and a small table had been prepared for them in the recently mown field. Several large, rough-thatched haystacks now stood in the meadow behind them.

"Have a seat Clive... tea?"

Wingood nodded as he sat down and Antrobus poured the tea.

"This is very nice Jack," he smiled as he looked about him.

Antrobus nodded.

"Aye, well, I thought we'd need a little sunshine... considering what we are going to talk about..."

Wingood frowned.

"The book you mean. The... Mysterious Worms?

"*Mysteries of the Worm*..." Antrobus corrected him, suddenly serious. "Aye..."

Wingood shifted nervously in his chair not certain he wanted to know much more.

"When we last spoke on the phone, you told me that you and... er... Dennis... had found something... something useful?"

Antrobus nodded.

"Aye, we did. But it was an unpleasant labour I don't mind telling you..." Antrobus' face darkened, and he looked away. "There are some things in this world Clive... and" he added in an undertone, "*beyond*... that it's best not to know about. Dennis told me it was written by a man called Ludvig Prinn, a sixteenth century necromancer and an all-round nasty piece of work apparently, who, had an all-round nasty end, when he was burnt at the stake for sorcery. Dennis didn't know too much about him, but he had heard of this book, he reckoned it was very rare and *very* sought after... in the right circles. I tell you, that first day when I placed it on the counter of his bookshop, well, the man was like a kid at bloody Christmas. I won't reveal the obscene amount of money he offered me for it, but he's welcome to the bloody thing ... I wouldn't want to keep it in my 'ouse..."

Antrobus looked up and shook his head slowly.

"Like I said," he murmured. "It was an unpleasant labour... though young Dennis was a good work mate."

Wingood sipped at his tea, but he carefully kept his gaze on Antrobus.

"On the first night we got to work," Antrobus continued, "Dennis started by telling me that we would have to tread slowly and carefully if we were going to read this thing without inviting great danger. Of course, I bowed to his knowledge and experience and so we cracked on only as fast as Dennis dared, each night translating small select sections and never, ever, reading anything aloud.

"And so, it went on. Dennis had his bookshop business to run in the day and I kept myself busy. I spent many hours in the Minster Library and the King's Manor Library, you know, research like. But I also spent time just being a tourist, taking a cruise down the Ouse, having a cup of tea and a sandwich in a café, or eating a pie and quaffing a couple of pints in a fine old Yorkshire hostelry. But each evening, just before seven, I would make my way to his home on Gudrumsgate Lane, a house as old as the dark book we were studying.

"Dennis and I spent hours each night, high up in his

draughty garret study, pouring over the weird old book and surrounded by other, equally strange old volumes. This was Dennis' 'special collection', and those books filled the leaning walls of the room ominously. He told me the library was largely inherited from his father, a French Canadian academic and a man who had apparently been an expert on the occult. And it seems that Dennis has continued the strange de Clerc academic tradition up there in Yorkshire…

"At any rate, we found what we were looking for at last. It's a ceremony of sealing. It's a way to…" he paused for a moment. "When the entity… the thing lurking beyond, when it comes, and if we do this right, then we can… hold it… or send it back… at least that's the theory…"

Wingood shook his head uncertainly.

"Do you think this… invocation… will work? Look what happened to those Germans your friend Manfred told you about… I'm not sure about this mumbo-jumbo stuff, I mean really, it seems so preposterous!"

Antrobus raised an eyebrow.

"Mumbo-jumbo? Well, what about that mumbo-jumbo you and your fellow masons get up to at the lodge… Seems like it's fine and dandy when it's safe and familiar."

Wingood frowned.

"That's not the same and you know it…" he sighed as he sipped his tea. Then, feeling a sudden inspiration, he sat up straight in his chair.

"Why don't we just blow it up? After all, you said yourself that you could get some dynamite…"

Antrobus nodded and smiled.

"Aye, I did, didn't I..."

But now he shook his head.

"No, it's a risk but we 'ave to do this properly. Dennis was insistent on that. 'Whatever you're up to,' he warned me, 'Make sure you follow the invocation *exactly*'..."

Wingood mopped the growing perspiration from his brow with his handkerchief.

"Well, it sounds bloody mad if you ask me..." was all he said.

Antrobus nodded once more.

"Aye, but the whole thing is bloody mad Clive, and if we get this wrong, well madness will be the least of our worries..."

Wingood swallowed uneasily. Then he said:

"Have you got it here then? The book I mean?"

But Antrobus shook his head.

"No, it's still in York... thank goodness," he replied. "I understand now why Manfred was so glad to be rid of it. Dennis has already found a buyer for it. I think he'll be able to retire early... but I hope the sale is soon, I don't like to think of that thing lying around his house..."

He seemed suddenly uneasy.

But Wingood looked at him puzzled.

"But the ceremony thing... how will you know what to do without the book?"

Antrobus waved his hand.

"Nay Clive, we don't need the bloody book. I *have* the invocation... and the instructions on its use... Dennis transcribed them for me."

He looked at Wingood sombrely.

"We're all set Clive... just about. I need to get a few more bits and pieces and then... well then, we *will* be ready... as ready as we can be..."

And so, Wingood had to reassume normality, at least for a few weeks more.

He did not plan to meet Antrobus again until the day of the solstice, but the two men spoke regularly on the telephone though their conversation rarely now touched on the task ahead of them.

In early June, Wingood announced to Antrobus that he was planning on taking Doris away on holiday for a few days. He would be back in time for the solstice. It had been Antrobus himself who had originally suggested the idea, and reluctantly Wingood had finally agreed.

"Have some time with your missus," Antrobus had encouraged him. "Before we have to, you know, get to work..."

Wingood arranged that an old golfing friend, another estate agent from nearby Hellsby, would 'caretake' some of his business during Wingood's absence, and provide cover on any property viewings. In exchange, Wingood would later return the favour. With the business safe under Debbie's watchful eye, Wingood took two weeks off and booked a 'Bed and Breakfast' for five days near Lake Windermere. Doris was delighted by the prospect and Wingood had not wanted her to be disappointed. He spared no expense, they completed every conceivable day trip, dined at up-market restaurants and Wingood even encouraged Doris *and* accompanied her when she wanted to go shopping at the market.

All in all, the holiday was a tremendous success with Doris. For poor Wingood, it was a living nightmare. Each smile was forced; each exclamation at the beauty of the landscape, false; each bite of food tasteless. Wingood was in an agony of expectation and suspense. Every morning, he crossed off the date in his pocket calendar, willing the solstice to arrive whilst simultaneously feeling nauseous with fear. He lost weight, but Doris only took this as a further sign that Wingood had turned over a new leaf. She was more content than she had been in years. And for that, at least, Wingood *was* glad.

CHAPTER FIVE
THE SOLSTICE

On the day of the solstice, Antrobus and Wingood had agreed to meet at Shippen Farm at eight o'clock sharp. But Wingood was late and, by the time he finally drew up in his Jaguar, it was already half-past nine.

"Good morning Jack... I'm sorry I'm late but... I'm sure that... well, someone's been following me... I think."

Antrobus could see that the other man was in a parlous state of nervous tension. Unspeaking, he drew Wingood inside and, despite Wingood's protestations that it was still too early in the morning, he fixed them both a stiff drink. They clinked their glasses and after downing his drink, Antrobus had busied himself with packing their equipment whilst Wingood paced about nervously.

Finally, Antrobus replied to Wingood's opening statement, though still seemingly absorbed in sorting through the equipment.

"So? Following you, were they?"

"Yes! Wingood insisted. "And it's not the first time I've thought so!" he drained his glass agitatedly. "Twice now I've seen a car following behind me." He frowned now in obvious frustration. "I could *tell* they were following me, I turned off several times, but they were *always* there..."

Apparently, he explained, only this morning, he had been forced to take a long circuitous route in order to elude his latest pursuer.

Antrobus was now wondering if he should be concerned by Wingood's seemingly increasing paranoia. It certainly ate at his own confidence somewhat. The old man grunted again in reply but, despite his growing concern for his friend, he was still unable to resist teasing him.

"'appen you're right," he replied, now lifting the duffle-bag and carrying it into his study. "It's most probably the police."

"The police!" Wingood suddenly exclaimed following the man into the room. In shock, he slowly placed the now empty glass back down on the coffee table.

"After all," Antrobus continued, pretending to still be absorbed with the contents of the duffle bag, "you're bound to be a suspect in the Marchley Howe case... You 'ave to be the *prime* suspect."

Wingood now looked aghast as he sank into a chair.

"Do you really think so?" he said anxiously. Then, as if to himself, he added, "I suppose Carruthers *was* trying to warn me..."

"Don't be such a daft bloody apeth!" Antrobus retorted

looking up at him now and laughing. "I'm only pulling your leg…They've got *nowt* on you Clive. They're out of their depth, even if they don't know it. Mayhap we'll be out of our depth too, soon enough…"

Then he looked at Wingood keenly as he straightened up, all humour now suddenly gone.

"Are you sure you are ready?"

Wingood nodded dumbly.

"I think so," he finally answered.

"Want some more Dutch courage?" Antrobus said, now offering a hip flask to Wingood. "It's a nice single malt?"

Wingood smiled weakly.

"No thanks. I'd better not have any more… I want to keep as clear a head as possible."

Antrobus shrugged.

"Suit yourself," he said, and he took a deep pull of the whisky. Then, he hefted the duffle-bag onto his shoulder with a grunt.

"Right then, let's go. And we'll take *my* car…"

They packed Antrobus' ancient Land Rover carefully. In the hall, stood a final bulky item, concealed by a black canvas tarpaulin. This object required them both to lift it into the boot. Wingood asked Antrobus what it was.

"A winch," the old man answered. "It runs on petrol and with this we can get back up that 'ole much quicker…"

Despite the warmth of the summer's morning, Wingood felt a shiver run up his spine.

At last, all was ready, and they set off, Antrobus now behind the wheel.

"We're a bit like Sherlock Holmes and Dr. Watson..." Wingood opined wanly, as they drove slowly through the dappled sunlight of the woody lane. "Off on another investigation..." He stared up at the sunlight, so bright and warm, but, he remembered, the eclipse was coming.

Antrobus grunted.

"Holmes and Watson?" he said drily. "More like bloody Abbot and Costello if you ask me..."

Their journey was soon completed without incident. The Wednesday morning traffic was mercifully light, and Antrobus was as certain as he could be that they were definitely not being followed. Once Wingood had opened and closed the tall iron gates after the car, they drove in silence as they approached the house. Marchley Howe sat before them like a jewel in a green velvet setting, beautiful, yet, Wingood now knew, rotten at its heart.

Neither man spoke as the engine died. Quickly, they unloaded the battered Land Rover and grunting with the effort, they carried everything to the rear of the house.

Wingood was forced to scramble through the window once more and, on Antrobus' instruction, he unbolted the old door to the former kitchen garden.

"No sense in trying to lift this through the window," Antrobus had stated pointing at the heavy hoist.

Sweating and puffing, the two men staggered through the kitchen area with their burdens. They made their way to the entrance hall and stopped for a breather, placing the equipment carefully down. Bright sunlight was once more streaming across the red tiles of the floor.

Mopping his brow Wingood stared at the cellar door nervously.

"This is it then," he mumbled.

With no little effort, they began to haul everything down the old stone steps into the now brightly illuminated crypt below.

Antrobus paused to examine the diesel generator.

Then, nodding to himself he said:

"Easy enough to fire this thing up if we need to. Von Hallerstein seemed to think that light was important so we'll 'ave to assume that he was right..." He tapped the top of the generator thoughtfully. "Right then... let's get to work."

Wingood looked at his watch. They still had three hours until the eclipse itself. With some further effort, they carried everything through to the last chamber. Antrobus positioned the hoist near to the wide dark mouth of the well.

"Do you feel that" Wingood whispered, his hand extended out over the opening. "I can feel a draft..." then, he suddenly wrinkled his nose in disgust, "Phew! And that smell...like a blocked drain..."

He turned away and wretched a little.

Antrobus raised an eyebrow.

"Are you sure you don't want a drop of Scotch, Clive?"

Wingood wiped his mouth with his handkerchief.

"I'm alright... God that was *vile*..." he looked at the hole again doubtfully. "Are you sure we have to go down there? Can't we just do the hocus-pocus thing here?"

"No Clive," Antrobus muttered as he now rummaged

through the duffle bag. "We need to be in that cave at the end of the tunnel. That's where they found von Hallerstein's blood, and his chalk circle. That's where he must have thought he needed to be to... to make contact... Why else would he have gone down there?"

He pulled a thick jumper from the bag and a brown woollen balaclava.

"Here, put these on... put the balaclava on under your helmet, you'll be glad of it soon enough."

Wingood lifted the huge, thickly knitted brown jumper and, removing his tweed jacket, drew it on. Then he pulled his jacket back on over the bulky woollen mass of the jumper. Self-consciously, he donned the balaclava then placed the miner's helmet on top.

"Aye, pretty as a picture Clive..." Antrobus remarked before pulling another jumper and a green balaclava out of the bag.

After he had put these items on, Antrobus continued to lay out the equipment and then secured the heavy, petrol-powered hoist, firmly to a stone pillar.

"It's a bit of a custom job... the main part of it used to be on my tractor... I've added this..."

Antrobus held up what looked like another walkie-talkie but this one had been clearly modified and was wrapped in black electrical tape.

"Radio remote control," he explained, "my own design. We can pull ourselves up as quick as a flash with this... if we 'ave to..."

Wingood shook his head.

"Are you sure it's safe?" he asked looking at the mass of wires sticking out of the receiver attached to the motor of the winch.

Antrobus nodded his head vigorously.

"Aye of course it is Clive. Don't forget, you'll be well strapped in and if the winch fails... which it won't..." he added quickly, "you can still stop yourself and hoist yourself up without it. It will just make things a little easier... for you."

Wingood looked at the older man fretfully.

"Can we just get this over with," he said, sighing.

"You first Clive, let's get you into this harness."

"Me... first?" Wingood said his face now paling. "Shouldn't I go last?" he looked at the nearby opening and shivered.

"No," Antrobus said firmly. "I'm going to lower you down slowly with the winch, I'll get you down there slow and safe and sound..."

Wingood allowed Antrobus to help him climb into his harness. Then, after attaching the rope through a series of clips and hoops, he stood back.

"Right, I'll just take up the slack," Antrobus said, slowly winding the rope back on the winch.

"Just stand over there, near to the edge," he instructed Wingood. "That's it, just like you saw me do last time... lean out... it'll easily take the weight."

Closing his eyes and desperately trying to stop himself from shaking, Wingood leaned slowly back, the harness and rope taut before him.

"Take a step Clive," Antrobus said encouraging him. "Walk it nice and slow." Had Wingood but known it, this was the part of their task that Antrobus had been worrying about the most. If he could get Wingood safely to the bottom, well, then the rest of the things could follow as they liked.

To Antrobus' relief, Wingood began his descent without incident. Antrobus lowered the rope slowly, controlling the winch manually. Everything went well, but he was still thankful to hear the walkie-talkie finally crackle into life.

"I'm here!" Wingood said still breathless from the descent. "Oh my God, it's horrible down here, the cold... and the *smell*..."

Antrobus stopped the winch and quickly picked up the other walkie-talkie.

"Hello Clive, unclip yourself from the rope. Over."

He could hear rustling and fumbling sounds over the radio receiver.

"Right, I'm free..." Wingood finally said, his voice tremulous with fear. "Are you coming? I don't mind telling you I don't want to be alone down here...er, o... over."

Antrobus nodded.

"On my way Clive, 'old on. Stand ready. Over."

He flicked on the light of his helmet and slung the duffle bag over his chest. Then, he placed the walkie talkie on the ground next to the winch and began the motor once more. The loud rattle of the petrol engine soon echoed around the chamber. Checking the fuel level in the custom winch and then that the radio remote was working once more, he finally climbed into his own harness and began to abseil down.

Wingood was relieved to see him when Antrobus reached the bottom of the well. Once Antrobus was free of his harness, the two men stepped quickly over the rubble and the remnants of ancient timbers. It was clear that these had tumbled down when the pit had been opened by von Hallerstein. Gradually, they made their way towards the entrance to the tunnel.

"This one's not as big as the one Manfred saw in Bolivia," Antrobus said, still clearly awed by the ancient structure, "but by 'eck, it's extraordinary."

Antrobus shone his light around the great, circular entrance of the tunnel.

Wingood looked about him uncomfortably. He was shaking due to both the intense cold and his increasingly frayed nerves.

Slowly, they began to walk into the tunnel itself and cautiously picked their way onwards, the distant clattering sound of the petrol winch fading into the darkness behind them.

The tunnel was much longer than Wingood had assumed, but it travelled onwards in a fairly level manner, and it was free from all debris and any signs of damage as far as Wingood could see. Only a thin layer of dry dust and dirt covered the floor, otherwise it seemed as intact as if it had only recently been constructed. Wingood stared up uneasily at the huge, flat interlocking sarsens that formed the walls of the spiralling edifice. Then the light of their lamps passed at last into night, and they recognised that they had reached the vast, final chamber itself.

Antrobus walked steadily up to the end of the tunnel and lay the olive duffle bag on the ground before turning back to Wingood.

"Just 'ere I reckon... what do you think? The floor is clear of any dust..."

Wingood shook his head as he uneasily advanced to the edge of the cavern's entrance.

"I don't know Jack, whatever you think..." he said still staring out into the gulf beyond.

"I wonder why there's no sign of the circle von Hallerstein made...? I mean, it should be here... shouldn't it?"

Antrobus shrugged.

"Maybe the old bill cleaned it all up... I don't ruddy know..."

Antrobus looked at his watch.

"Plenty of time yet, at any rate," he announced quietly, as he began to lay out the contents of the duffle bag.

Wingood shivered.

"Can I do anything to help?" he offered.

But Antrobus only shook his head as he busied himself.

"Keep moving, keep warm, have a bit of a look about," he suggested. "See if you can make owt out."

Reluctantly Wingood agreed and began to investigate the cave uncertainly.

"Alright..." he said, "but I'm not going far..."

Then he began to explore the empty chamber.

He saw that it was just as Antrobus had originally

described it, vast, black and seemingly empty of anything at all. There were no rocks or debris on the smooth floor there was even no sign of the ever-present film of dust and dirt that they had seen in the tunnel. But just as Antrobus had said, there was a *feeling* here, a *nasty* feeling. Wingood shuffled slowly to the nearest wall, shining his lamp onto the smooth glass-like surface of the domed chamber. Then, suddenly curious he pointed his lamp upwards. At the edge of the light's reach, perhaps forty or fifty feet above the level of the floor, he thought he could see a break in the blank smoothness of the walls. He squinted and shifted the light about, trying to see more clearly. Then he realised what he was looking at. There were holes up there, dozens of circular holes no bigger than a handsbreadth but pitting the wall uniformly, like some kind of dark honeycomb, high up wherever he shone his light along the gallery's walls. He imagined those strange holes rising and covering the smooth dome of the chamber as well.

With that unnerving discovery, Wingood made his way quickly back to the other man.

"This place... feels... well... wrong," he muttered shaking his head and glancing at his own watch anxiously. "There are a lot of holes, all about the walls. It gave me the creeps I don't mind telling you."

Antrobus grunted but did not look up. Wingood watched as Antrobus began to lay a variety of objects onto the cavern floor.

Finally, Antrobus turned to Wingood.

"Help me draw the circle... from here to here, but we mustn't close it, not yet."

Wingood nodded dumbly as Antrobus handed him a long thin stick with a large piece of chalk attached to the end.

"It's a hazel wand," he explained. "You start on this side, and I'll do the other, we'll meet in the middle."

Silently shaking from the cold and the dreadful suspense, the two men slowly transcribed a wide circle on the bare floor just outside the entrance to the cavern. They stopped when there was only a two-foot unmarked space remaining.

Antrobus stood up straight and placed his own stick on the floor.

"Right, we will only enter and leave the circle here." He turned to Wingood, "And Clive, it's vitally important that you remember not to step over the line anywhere else, not now and especially not during the ritual."

Wingood nodded but could not help shivering again at the word 'ritual'.

Then, Antrobus picked up a long black box. He slowly walked around the inside of the circle, withdrawing tall thick candles from the box as he went, and setting them at four regular points on the circle's circumference.

Next, Antrobus began to draw another circle inside the outer one. This he soon completed. Then he pulled something from inside his jacket pocket. It was a thin cardboard cylinder that Antrobus now opened at one end. He pulled out a paper scroll and seemed to examine it carefully.

THE HORROR BENEATH

Retrieving his chalk wand, he began to draw strange, angular markings onto the floor.

Antrobus drew a character at the point of each of the candles. Then, seemingly satisfied, he moved carefully back out of the circle and returned his attention back to the duffle bag.

To Wingood's surprise, Antrobus now withdrew a large white garment that he folded carefully and placed on top of the duffle bag.

"Is that a priest's surplice!" Wingood asked in amazement. "Where on earth did you get that from."

Antrobus winked at him.

"Never mind that," he said now pulling out a long, richly decorated, purple stole and placing it on top of the surplice. "This stole has been blessed by the Bishop of Deva himself, I reckon it won't do us any harm to have something holy with us. If all goes well, I'll make sure I get it back to the vicar I borrowed it from..."

Shaking his head in surprise Wingood was more excited when he saw the next item Antrobus produced. It was a large flask.

"How about a nice cup of tea whilst we wait, eh?"

Wingood actually smiled then, despite their cold, and dismal surroundings.

"Oh, you're a bloody marvel Jack!" he exclaimed.

Smiling a little himself, Antrobus proceeded to unscrew the top of the flask and poured out the tea into two tin mugs. Then, before Wingood could protest, he poured a generous measure of the whisky from his hip flask into each cup.

Wingood took the hot tea thankfully, and, seated with Antrobus on the floor just outside of the circle, he sipped at the sweet, hot brew, now gratefully enjoying the unfamiliar but quickly warming, combination of whisky and tea.

"How long have we got," he said at length as Antrobus refilled their mugs.

Antrobus sniffed and looked at his watch.

"Still another hour Clive."

They sat shivering on the edge of the cavern and waited. Somewhere, far above their heads in the bright, midsummer's sky, the moon crept towards its inevitable dark assembly with the sun.

The minutes passed slowly, both men occasionally rising to stamp their feet and walk about in order to keep their circulation going and to shake off the creeping, numbing cold. They had just finished having a smoke with the last of the tea when Antrobus suddenly stiffened and, pushing his pipe back into his pocket, quickly set his tin mug aside.

"Clive! It's getting colder!" he exclaimed.

Wingood jumped in fright.

"Come on, get into the circle, it's nearly time," Antrobus ordered, standing once more whilst now glancing at his watch.

As Wingood retreated into the circle, Antrobus quickly pulled on the white surplus over his jacket. Then he settled the embroidered stole over his shoulders.

"You look every inch the fine ecclesiastical gentleman... except for the balaclava and miner's helmet..." Wingood said with a weak smile. He stood there, a bent form in the dim light of his lamp, shivering with fear.

Antrobus gave him half a smile as he re-entered the circle.

"Aye Clive, 'appen I do"

He lifted the chalk wand and turned to face Wingood.

"Right, I'm going to seal it up. Remember, don't leave the circle until it's all over... or I..." he paused and then setting his jaw squarely said, "At any rate, *whatever 'appens*, stay inside the circle!" With a steely look he lay a hand on Wingood's shoulder. "When this begins well, who knows what's coming. But remember, the eclipse will only last for about seven minutes. That's when it will try and come through. Just seven minutes, that's all we need to hold on for."

Taking up the wand, Antrobus drew the chalk circle closed. Then, turning to the darkness he solemnly intoned:

"Now let it work. Mischief, thou art afoot. Take thou what course thou wilt."

Wingood turned to look at him.

"Is that part of the spell thing?" he whispered, hoarse now with awe and fright.

Antrobus continued to stare out into the darkness before them, but he smiled once more.

"Nay Clive, it's just another bit of old Billy Shakespeare..."

He now reached into his pocket and carefully pulled out

the scroll. Studying it once more, he pulled out his lighter and walking clockwise around the circle, lit each of the candles in turn, starting with the northernmost candle.

"Right," he said. "The circle is sealed, come... what may."

The two men stared at each other and to Wingood's surprise, Antrobus extended his hand. They shook hands in silence, Wingood trembling like a leaf in a spring breeze, Antrobus looking sombre but steady.

"According to this," Antrobus now said. "There will come a point when... this Black Worm or whatever it is, will approach and attempt to... move *through* the seal and disrupt the banishing that we are trying to create..." He looked at Wingood. "This is key Clive, this is *why* you had to be here, with me. *You* have to draw the final symbol, when I tell you, whatever else is happening, *you* just make sure you draw this shape."

He passed the scroll to Wingood who stared at the strange angular letter that Antrobus was pointing to.

Wingood nodded, clutching his hazel rod and chalk tightly.

"Right... good man," Antrobus looked at his watch again. "It must be only moments now... Get ready Clive." He shone his lamp out into the dark void before them. "If anything is going to happen," he looked at his watch again, "the eclipse is starting... it's about to happen... now."

Suddenly, the cold deepened and Wingood could no longer feel the end of his nose. Then came the sound. It boomed across the cavern with a physical force that staggered the men. Deep and bass and utterly overwhelming.

The throbbing depths of the cacophony swept over them in waves.

Wingood, fell to his knees, his hands clasped to his ears, crying out in torment.

"I can feel it... it's in my bloody head. It's the bloody German artillery!"

"Get a grip on yourself man!" Antrobus shouted, his own face contorted in pain by the psychic, aural assault. "Try to resist it... and stay in the bloody circle!"

Even as the two men writhed in shock and pain, something began to swell and form at the very centre of the cavernous space before them.

It began as a swirling flux made of some sluggish, viscous light. Then, pulsing unnaturally, it grew rapidly larger. Burning with a cold luminescence, the entity continued to coalesce before them.

Now Wingood screamed out in horror.

"What in God's name is it?" he gasped, feeling the bile rising in his throat.

Antrobus did not answer, stricken mute by an overpowering, preternatural dread.

The expanding materialisation, began to exude long, wriggling tendrils of a sickly, lambent hue. These glowing appendages whipped and probed the air, ever expanding.

Wingood watched in disgust, as dozens of black, elliptical discs, suddenly materialised at the very top of the pulsating form. Framed by the sickly light, the groups swivelled and then, blinking, seemed to regard the two men. Wingood shuddered, feeling the scrutiny of the myriad, black clusters. These were indeed its eyes. Wingood vomited but his loud gagging was joined by the sudden cry of a man's voice, almost inaudible in the spectral din.

Antrobus, his arms raised in the air was shouting words, strange arcane words that Wingood could not understand but which he knew were Latin.

The candles flared brightly and Antrobus gasped suddenly winded, but the circle held, and the terrible roaring sound stopped abruptly. But it was replaced by a ghastly, foetid wind that whipped at them and moaned through the air.

Panting with effort, Antrobus regained his feet and helped pull Wingood back up from the floor.

Now the creature began to exude a new, longer shining pseudopod towards them, but the end of this one began to protrude and swell grotesquely, like a monstrous snail's eyestalk. They could not bear to look nor could they tear their gaze away, as the thing continued to expand and grow repulsively. Gradually, dangling in the air at the end of the waving tentacle, a physical mass began to form. They watched stricken, as something twisted and wriggled inside the expanding, slick sack that hung from the long glowing member. And slowly, as it continued to pulse and lengthen, they could finally see what it was.

"Oh my God, my God..." Wingood shouted, crying out with both shock and disgust. "It's von Hallerstein! And... oh Christ...!" Wingood cried in revulsion, "He's bloody screaming!"

Both men still stared, unable to look away from the

dangling, twisting figure of the man imprisoned inside the glutinous cocoon. Von Hallerstein's body squirmed, supported by dozens of ribbed and pulsing tubes, that seemed to pierce his flesh at several points. But his eyes were worst of all, rolling in his head, as the figure continued to scream in mute agony.

Then, von Hallerstein's palsied, naked body, jerked stiffly. And a moment later, they heard, over the maelstrom of unearthly wailing, a discordant voice, hissing and gurgling from von Hallerstein's foaming and contorted mouth. But it was not von Hallerstein that spoke.

"*Let me pass. My time is come,*" the voice commanded.

Antrobus looked stricken and stared at the circle about them. More tendrils of eldritch light began to form that now reached out to the men in the circle.

"Draw the sigil Clive!" Antrobus shouted desperately. "Do it now!"

But the estate agent stood unmoving, petrified with terror, skin crawling and hair standing on end, as the aberrant thing drew ever closer.

"*Let me passsss. My time is come,*" von Hallerstein's body jerked like a puppet, his lips forming the words awkwardly, painfully, as the thing shimmered viscously towards them.

"Bloody hell Clive! Draw it now!"

Moved by the desperation of Antrobus' shouted command, Wingood looked back, wide-eyed. Then, with slow, shakingly ponderous steps, he stumbled to the very centre of the circle. With quaking hands, he bent and tried to pick up the wand, but it fell from his grasp and clattered back to the ground. The stick of chalk cracked off and Wingood watched dazedly as it rolled quickly away across the circle.

Eyes fixed on the entity, Antrobus let out another yell of horror, then in a cracked, strained voice, began reciting again in Latin, but now Wingood dared not look. He propelled himself forwards clumsily, and, falling flat on the floor, slapped at the chalk before it rolled out of the circle. Clasping it in his palsied grasp, tears streaming from his eyes, and now sobbing uncontrollably, he crawled to the centre of the circle and painstakingly inscribed the sigil onto the floor.

Wingood was unsure what he had expected to happen, but this was not it. The silence collapsed on them like a sudden weight and Wingood fell flat on the floor, simply trying to breathe, he *must* breathe. Antrobus was silent, lying prone nearby. Slowly and shakily, Wingood pulled himself up to his feet. The cold! The cold was *gone*. Wiping tears from his eyes and sniffing, he reluctantly shone his light outwards. Wingood stared as the thin beam reached into the emptiness before him. Nothing... But then he stopped. No, not quite empty. Something was lying on the floor, just on the edge of his light. Something glistening and dark. Dazedly, he turned now to Antrobus and checked his pulse. Then, not knowing what to do he shook the other man's shoulders roughly. Suddenly remembering the hip flask, he pushed the surplice aside and reached into the old man's pocket. He pulled the silver flask out, opened it and pressed it quickly to Antrobus's lips. With a choking explosion of whisky, the old man opened his eyes and gave a great hacking cough.

"Bloody hell Clive, are you trying to kill me?"

He put his hand to his mouth and coughed again as he sat up quickly.

"What's 'appening? Where is it?" he said looking about wildly.

Wingood looked at him and shook his head.

"It's gone... I think we might have done it," was all he could manage.

Antrobus, groaning, stood to his feet and looked at his watch. But it had stopped, and the glass was shattered. The place was now deathly quiet. Antrobus reached down and retrieved the now crumpled incantation from the floor.

"I need to burn this," he muttered. "Dennis said that would be the final act."

Quickly, he pulled his zippo lighter from his pocket and lit the flame.

The two men watched as the paper burned to grey ash at their feet.

"I thought I saw something just now..." Wingood suddenly remembered. "Over there, on the floor of the cavern..." he whispered.

Antrobus squinted, pointing his light into the darkness. He too, thought he could make something out, lying on the floor of the cave. He frowned and turned to Wingood.

"Aye, 'appen you're right..." he said, thoughtfully. "At any rate, I reckon we can leave the circle now Clive... Let's take a look before we get out of here."

"Wait," Wingood said holding Antrobus' sleeve. "Do you think it is safe? Is it over?"

Antrobus shrugged.

"How should I know?" he answered with a sudden smile. "We're still alive, aren't we?"

With a final glance at each other, the two men stepped in tandem out of the circle. They stood for a moment in silence, trying to collect themselves once more. Then, slowly, they turned and began to walk across the dark, echoing space.

"Hold on Clive..." Antrobus said as they neared the dark shape. To Wingood's surprise, Antrobus pulled an old service revolver from an inside pocket. Then, cautiously, the writer approached the shape.

"Bloody Hell!" Antrobus suddenly cried, bending down.

Wingood jumped and took a step forward uncertainly.

"What is it? Jack, what have you found?"

But Antrobus only gestured for him to come closer and see.

Then Wingood saw.

Lying across a gelatinous pool was a torn, slick membrane. Partially covered with the sticky substance lay the naked body of von Hallerstein.

The two men stared speechless, then, crouching slowly down, Antrobus reached a tentative hand to grasp von Hallerstein's wrist.

After a moment, he suddenly shouted out.

"He's alive! I've got a bloody pulse."

Wingood staggered over, his eyes wide with shock and disbelief.

"Come on Clive, give me a hand…"

Antrobus began to pull von Hallerstein's limp form free of the blubbery dissolving mass that encased him.

With a great effort, between them they managed to drag von Hallerstein's unconscious body back towards the tunnel. When they reached the circle, Antrobus turned to Wingood and said:

"Let's cover him in the surplice, that will be easiest, and he'll be a bit warmer…"

They awkwardly managed to pull the surplice over the unconscious von Hallerstein's head. Antrobus then looked quickly about him and grabbing the duffle bag, pulled it over his shoulder. Now straining with the weight, the two men began to carry von Hallerstein back along the tunnel, his feet dragging in the dust in their wake.

"What about all the rest of your stuff?" Wingood asked presently, now out of breath and looking over his shoulder as they slowly made their way back down the tunnel with their burden.

Antrobus shook his head.

"I'll get it later, come on, let's get him to an 'ospital."

With an effort, they finally reached the base of the pit, and, after a short breather, the two men managed to harness von Hallerstein's prone body onto the winch-rope. The German now hung from the harness like a collapsed marionette. Satisfied, Antrobus turned back to Wingood.

"He's an old soldier too Clive. Did you see the blood type

tattoo under his arm? He was once batting for the other side" He smiled grimly then took hold of his own rope. "I'm going up as well, one of us needs to be at the top to get his body out of the harness... I'll be as quick as I can, though I don't mind telling you I am a bit done-in..."

He looked up at the distant light.

"At least the lights are still on, and I can hear the winch's motor running..."

Antrobus stopped speaking abruptly. The walkie-talkie around Wingood's neck had suddenly crackled into life.

Wingood, eyes widening in surprise, stared back at him in puzzlement. Then, before they could speak, they heard a man's voice bark out over the static.

"Hello, is there anyone down there? Over!"

"That's *my* walkie-talkie..." Antrobus said in a hoarse whisper. "someone's using the one I forgot up there by the winch!"

The two men stood and stared at the walkie-talkie that Wingood now held in his hand.

Wingood's mouth dropped open.

But Antrobus quickly snatched the walkie-talkie out of his hand. Ignoring Wingood's quiet protestation, he spoke into the radio.

"Hello, I'm sending up an injured man... be ready to receive him... Over."

He threw the walkie-talkie back to Wingood and pulled the custom radio controller from around his neck.

"Right, here goes."

They watched as the recumbent von Hallerstein rose smoothly into the dark passage above them.

After several expectant minutes the man's voice came out of the walkie-talkie once more.

"Package received. I'm sending the rope back down. Are you coming up? Over."

Antrobus looked at Wingood accusingly, but the estate agent only shrugged.

"I promise you; I don't know what's going on... do you think it's the police?"

"Well," Antrobus replied archly, "it's not my bloody Aunt Fanny!" He winked at Wingood. "There's one way to find out. Come on Clive let's hoist you up."

Wingood was soon ready to go and Antrobus pressed the radio remote once more. Slowly then more rapidly, Wingood began to ascend.

When he reached the top, he was momentarily blinded by the electric brightness of the crypt. Squinting now, he felt strong hands guide him up onto his feet.

"Hello Mr. Wingood, fancy meeting you here."

It was detective-inspector MacDonald.

Wingood blinked and stared at the policeman fearfully.

"Eh... er... what...? What are you doing here?"

MacDonald arched an eyebrow and pointed at von Hallerstein's recumbent form.

"I might ask you the same question..."

Deftly, he patted the dazed Wingood down for concealed weapons. Then he smiled at the estate agent.

"You can never be too sure, can you? Now, let's run the rope back down and see who else is down there, eh?"

Wingood watched as MacDonald released the rope and lowered it down.

They waited in silence as the winch began to pull up the rope once more.

"And which of the seven dwarves is this?" MacDonald said sarcastically, pulling out a pistol and training it at Antrobus as the old man now emerged exhausted and grimy from the well. Slowly, Antrobus unfastened his harness and shut off the noisy petrol winch.

"What's going on?" Antrobus asked, giving the armed man a hard stare.

MacDonald sighed still pointing the pistol.

"I'm a copper and I'll ask the questions grandad. Now answer me, who are you?"

Antrobus pulled the balaclava from his head roughly.

"My name's Antrobus... and you are?" he said crabbily.

Ignoring him, MacDonald moved over and quickly patted Antrobus down, keeping the pistol levelled at the old man as he did so.

"Huh ho!" he suddenly exclaimed pulling the revolver out of the inside pocket of Antrobus' jacket. "Got a licence for this have you?" he asked archly.

Antrobus looked at him defiantly but shook his head.

"No? I didn't think so..." MacDonald said.

He gestured with the pistol to Wingood to come and stand beside Antrobus.

"Now, listen carefully," he said when they both stood

before him. "I'm going to go back to my car to call an ambulance and some back-up on my radio. I won't be long, but I will be locking you in down here."

He looked at them gravely as he slowly began to retreat.

"It seems I was right about you Mr. Wingood... You know, I've been following you... unofficially of course... It was that day you came in with that letter from von Hallerstein, *that* was the first red flag!"

MacDonald smiled as he continued to back away.

"Hubris Mr. Wingood, you wouldn't believe how many villains I've caught because of hubris... Unfortunately, I was taken *off* the von Hallerstein case... much against my will." MacDonald's face twisted in frustration. "But I knew there was something going on and you *had* to be involved in it..."

"Wait detective!" Wingood protested. "You don't understand... we've just saved von Hallerstein...!"

"You're wasting your breath Clive," Antrobus said looking at the policeman contemptuously. "Inspector Lestrade here thinks Holmes and Watson are guilty."

MacDonald only smiled.

"I don't know what you two have been up to down there but I'm sure that between you, you can concoct an excellent alibi whilst I'm gone. In the meantime..."

The words died on the policeman's lips as, rising from the dark pit below came the sound of a distant and vague, musical piping.

Furrowing his brow, he pointed the gun once more at the two men.

"What the hell is that? What's that... noise?" his voice held a note of uncertainty that had not been present before.

But Wingood only blanched and fell back cringing against the wall of the crypt.

Nor did Antrobus at first reply. He stood, seemingly frozen with uncertainty.

Cautiously, MacDonald came back into the chamber and edged closer to the cavity. As he reached the lip, he glanced at the two men.

"What's that noise I said," he demanded angrily.

Then the sound came again, nearer now.

Wingood slid down the wall and sat in a heap on the floor.

"Oh God... it's back... it's only bloody back..."

MacDonald frowned and turned to Antrobus furiously.

"What's he going on about?" he thundered. Then he recoiled as a breeze wafted up into the chamber. "Oh bugger... What's that smell?"

He reeled away, then righting himself, turned to the well once more.

Now they could all hear it plainly, the echoes of the piping noise rising ever louder.

"This is something else," Antrobus hissed at last, his face pale and drawn. "I think *this* is the Black Worm...!"

Wingood was sobbing now, shaking his head in horror.

"I thought we stopped the entity... I thought..."

Antrobus, quickly pulled his stare from MacDonald.

"No Clive! This is *not* that entity..." he said emphatically, shaking Wingood's shoulders. "Or at least it's not a manifestation from beyond... like that *other* thing..." he suddenly spat. "I was a bloody fool Clive!" he cursed. "*This* is the old thing, some ancient, antediluvian monstrosity, the guardian of the deep, the guardian of the gateway, this is the Black Worm!"

Wingood suddenly giggled hysterically.

"I told you we would need some dynamite..." he said, wiping his sleeve across his face.

But Antrobus' eyes suddenly widened.

"Dynamite! You bloody genius Clive...! I'd forgotten..."

He turned then, and reaching into the duffle bag, desperately started rummaging inside.

"Oi! Old timer, get away from there!"

His attention torn between the hole and the two men on the other side, MacDonald now felt the rank breeze stiffen. Suddenly filled with a perilous curiosity, the tall policeman leaned over the edge and peered down into the black aperture.

He saw what was coming.

MacDonald's face twisted in fright. Instinctively, he raised the pistol and began firing. The booming explosion of echoing shots deafened them all. The roar of gunfire was followed by a slick, whipping sound, and a long, black and sinewy tentacle coiled itself tightly about MacDonald's right thigh.

With a scream, the man was dragged into the hole, his head slamming sickeningly onto the edge of the stonework as he fell.

"Judas Priest!" Antrobus exclaimed in shock.

Ears still ringing, he looked slowly down at the two taped clusters of dynamite sticks in his hand, then, reaching into his back pocket for his clasp knife, he cut both of the wicks in half.

Something was coming back up the well. The smell was suddenly overwhelming and besides the now ever-present outlandish piping, there was a growing rushing, gurgling and slapping sound.

"Clive!" Antrobus shouted, "Get out of here, take von Hallerstein and go!"

Wingood only stared at the other man dumbly.

With an anxious glance at the well, Antrobus turned to Wingood and kicked him hard.

"Come on Clive, time to go!"

Placing the dynamite on the floor, he dragged Wingood to his feet and, grunting with the effort, he pushed him across to von Hallerstein's unconscious body.

"Drag him out, just get out now!"

Without waiting to see whether Wingood was going, Antrobus bent down and quickly retrieved the dynamite. The rising smell from the hole was now nauseating, like rotting seaweed and fungal spoils.

Antrobus pulled out his lighter.

"Keep going Clive!" he shouted over his shoulder. "You've got less than ten seconds..."

Then he lit the two fuses and threw the bound sticks of dynamite into the hole before turning and running.

Antrobus dared a brief look back as he reached the arched exit. Even in the moment of that snatched glance, the lights now flickering and dimming, he had seen *something* had emerged, *flowing* upwards. Antrobus had had a vague impression of a dark, flopping, glistening mass. And then the lights had gone out completely. Yet, in that sudden darkness, for the briefest moment, he had realised with horror that he could see *inside* the thing. With a gasp of disgust, he saw MacDonald's dead face, weirdly illuminated by the glowing light of the waterproof fuses, as they all sank into the rising form of the black, misshapen creature. In quickening terror, Antrobus turned and ran for his life.

He saw Wingood's lamp some way ahead of him, he was moving slowly, dragging von Hallerstein's body along the flagstones of the undercroft.

Stumbling on in the darkness, Antrobus heard a sound like the crack of a bullwhip. He stumbled as something with a grip of iron coiled about his ankle. Even as he cried out in pain and despair, he heard a muffled crump, followed by a deafening roaring explosion. And then Antrobus knew no more.

Wingood was several strides ahead of Antrobus when the dynamite detonated. He thought he had heard something, something indescribably hideous before that sound was swallowed up by the sudden roar of the explosion. Wingood was thrown down on top of von Hallerstein whose prone body largely cushioned his fall. Dazed, but still conscious, he looked warily about him. The power was out, and his miner's helmet was gone but Wingood could still see. He turned and saw the glow of red flame through a thin gap in the rubble of the collapsed undercroft behind him. Thick clouds of choking dust and smoke billowed through the air. Turning now, Wingood finally spied Antrobus. The writer was lying in a bloody and crumpled heap by the dark base of the stone steps. He was about to call out to him when he stopped and sniffed. What was *that* smell... like fuel? He remembered the diesel generator and looked to the corner where it had stood. All that remained was a mangled heap of metal, crushed by a large piece of tumbled masonry. The fuel barrels had been scattered in the blast and several were leaking. That was what he could smell, he realised. Then he noticed the flow of the spilt fuel was pooling towards the back of the collapsed undercroft, where the fire was still burning...

He twisted quickly and tried to stand. His legs were wobbly, and he could feel something sticky and wet dribbling slowly down the side of his head, but he seemed otherwise unscathed.

"Jack!" he cried hoarsely shaking the prone figure. "Jack, wake up!"

He was relieved to see that his desperate calls and physical manhandling had had an immediate effect. Antrobus was now moving, his eyes opened.

"Bloody hell," he groaned rubbing his head gingerly. "What's going on Clive?"

Wingood smiled but he had tears in his eyes.

"We need to get out of here, the diesel, it's leaking... come on Jack get up."

Helping the old man to his feet they shambled slowly to the steps. Antrobus suddenly halted.

THE HORROR BENEATH

"Where's the Jerry?" he asked staggering slightly.

Wingood was about to answer when there was a whoosh of sudden flame.

"Jack, quick! Help me!"

The two men reached the unconscious von Hallerstein and, exhausted, they half carried, half dragged the German, up the old stone steps of the cellar.

They emerged at last into the entrance hall. The house was rapidly filling with a thick, roiling black smoke. Even as they stepped over the threshold there was a roar and a flash behind them. They were engulfed in a sudden sheet of fire that was quickly accompanied by the acrid smell of singed hair and smoking tweed.

"Ye Gods!" Antrobus cried, patting at the sleeves of his smouldering jacket. "The whole place is going up and us with it!"

Stumbling with hacking coughs, they struggled to find their way in the dense, dark smoke. Wingood and Antrobus dragged von Hallerstein between them. The kitchen was already in flames and scorched and blistered they beat a path to the back of the house. Just as they shut the heavy oak door of the passage, they heard the kitchen ceiling come tumbling in and there was a greedy roar of flames. Coughing and wheezing, they crashed out of the kitchen garden door and staggered, blackened and still smoking, away from the house. There was another shattering explosion from below as more of the diesel barrels ignited. This was quickly followed by a roaring, cacophonous crash of glass, masonry and timber. As they scrambled away, a climbing furnace engulfed Marchley Howe.

The two men, soot-blackened and ragged, sat on the ground at the edge of the drive, both stared at the burning remains of the house before them.

"Aye," Antrobus said at last, coughing. "That was unpleasant..."

Wingood now turned and gave the older man a disbelieving look.

"Unpleasant?" he gasped. "Unpleasant doesn't really sum it up for me... Poor MacDonald..."

Wingood shook his head dazedly.

"I still don't understand what that was. I don't quite... I..."

Antrobus coughed and spat on the floor.

"You'll be alright Clive," he said attempting to be reassuring, and patting Wingood on the shoulder. "You'll be alright. We're both old soldiers... Just like the lingering memory of the battlefield, you'll learn to deal with it. The sensation... should, eventually, fade."

But Wingood was filled with doubt. He knew that his life had changed forever.

Turning around, Antrobus now stared across to MacDonald's parked car. Von Hallerstein was lying, still unconscious, across the back seat.

Pulling his pipe from his pocket, Antrobus suddenly cursed as he saw that the stem had been broken in two.

Dropping the broken pieces to the floor, he turned back to Wingood.

"Have you any fags Clive?" he asked.

Wingood continued to stare ahead at the jagged remains of the house that now seemed crouched like a fiery, dying spider. Dazedly, his gaze still fixed on the collapsed, burning mass before him, he reached into the shredded and charred remains of his tweed jacket pocket and withdrew a crumpled pack of cigarettes that he thrust towards the old man.

Antrobus pulled out a bent cigarette and lighting it, sighed.

"Ta, very much" he said.

They sat in silence a moment longer.

"Ambulance and fire brigade should be here soon," Antrobus finally stated. "*And* the police... make sure you get the story straight Clive..."

Then, to Wingood's dazed surprise, Antrobus suddenly chuckled and, turning his gaze at last from the remains of Marchley Howe, Wingood turned to stare at his companion.

"Well," Antrobus said, winking slyly at him, "At least the Jerry is still breathing. You know what that means don't you?"

Wingood shook his head dumbly.

Antrobus smiled mischievously.

"Aye, well... As well as stopping some unspeakable evil, we are also three thousand quid better off. Not an entirely unprofitable evening."

Wingood had no answer to that.

Antrobus took a long pull on the cigarette.

"We could give the money to MacDonald's missus, if he has one."

Wingood nodded slowly.

"Yes..." he said distractedly. "That's a good idea..."

Antrobus flicked the cigarette end away.

"Oh, and Clive?"

"Yes," Wingood replied numbly.

Antrobus squeezed Wingood's shoulder and looked at him earnestly.

"The next time you sell a haunted house... Well... *don't* bloody well call me."

EPILOGUE

Clive Wingood had wandered awkwardly through the hospital ward. At last, after asking a passing nurse, he had been directed to von Hallerstein's bedside. The German was isolated, lying in a spartan and sterile room, a drip in his arm and his face drawn and grey. He had been asleep when Wingood entered and Wingood had draped his Macintosh over the back of a chair and sat down to wait, placing the brown paper bag of grapes that he had brought onto the small, wheeled table that stood next to the bed.

At last, von Hallerstein awoke and after some moments looked at Wingood and attempted to smile.

"Well, here you are at last Mr. Wingood," he finally said hoarsely, "And, I believe I am in your debt, for was it not you who found me?"

Wingood nodded his head as he sat awkwardly next to the hospital bed. Now he was slowly turning his flat cap with his hands, discomfited by von Hallerstein's visible decline.

There was a long awkward silence before von Hallerstein spoke again in a cracked, wheezing voice.

"Perhaps you would like to tell me... your story?" Von Hallerstein asked.

Wingood stared at von Hallerstein. The German was still emaciated and frail from his ordeal, all vitality seemed to have been *leached* out of him.

"If you are up to it?" he said uncertainly.

Von Hallerstein smiled weakly.

"I insist," he answered.

Clearing his throat, Wingood slowly began telling von Hallerstein a summary of the events of the past few months and their culmination at Marchley Howe.

When the tale was recounted, von Hallerstein sighed and lay his head back on his pillow, staring up at the white ceiling.

"Then I am truly in your debt Mr. Wingood, it seems that I owe you my life..."

Wingood blushed a little.

"What was it like?" he finally asked, reticently. "Where did you go... when that... thing... took you?"

But von Hallerstein only shook his head, his dark eyes flashing now with remembered pain.

"That memory I must try to seal forever... it is... not something I ever wish to revisit, only madness lies there..."

Wingood saw von Hallerstein's face crease in pain once

more and he remained quiet for a minute. Then he asked a question that had been nagging at his mind.

"The German expedition to Bolivia, in the thirties... who was *that* von Hallerstein?"

Von Hallerstein sighed deeply.

"That, my dear Wingood, was my father."

He now looked at Wingood earnestly.

"My mother was only informed that he had died in Bolivia in the service of the Reich," he sighed again. "I eventually inherited both my father's title and his arcane legacy... That is all that I will say."

Von Hallerstein looked at the carafe of water next to the bed.

"Would you mind?"

Standing quickly, Wingood poured a glass of water and passed it to the patient.

Von Hallerstein drank deeply and then with trembling hand, set the glass down.

"What have you told the police?" he asked after a moment.

Wingood frowned and looked about him nervously.

"I told them that I had simply gone to the house to ensure that all was still well with the property When I arrived, I had found the house ablaze and you, gravely ill, but still alive. I said I placed you in the policeman's car and called the police. I subsequently explained to them... several times... that your presence there, and the whereabouts of detective-inspector MacDonald, were both a complete mystery to me... I think... that they believed me in the end," he grimaced uncomfortably.

"The other chap, Jack Antrobus is his name, well he and I agreed on the same story beforehand. He told them that as a local farmer, he'd been interested in taking over the maintenance contract on the land. And, as I was the last estate agent who had dealt with those matters, he had obviously turned to me for advice."

Von Hallerstein listened patiently as Wingood recited his 'alibi'. Then Wingood frowned.

"The doctor told me that you probably had something called, dissociative amnesia?"

Von Hallerstein smiled grimly.

"That is because I have told the doctor that I can remember nothing of my ordeal. But I only wish it were true..."

The men lapsed into silence for a few moments. Then Wingood set his cap down on his lap.

"It is... over now, isn't it?" he said at last in a low voice. "I mean, the... the thing... the things... they're not coming back... are they?"

Von Hallerstein, nodded his head weakly.

"Yes, I think it is over," he replied in that croaking whisper. "My presence here confirms it. You did well, you and this fellow Antrobus. You 'removed' it, and I... well, I suppose that, as I was not part of the banishment, I *remained*."

He winced again and closed his eyes.

"As for that other thing... well fire and crushing rock

seem to have done their work... so all is cleansed and sealed you might say. But the presence of that gateway, like a deep stain, will linger for many, many years." Von Hallerstein coughed painfully and frowned. "No, such a thing does not abide for any time without leaving a shadow of its occupation... I am, unfortunately, only too aware of that truth."

Now he turned and looked at Wingood earnestly. To Wingood's surprise von Hallerstein suddenly reached out a thin arm and grasped the sleeve of the other man's jacket.

"There is one thing that you still must do Wingood," his eyes flashed again but now with a sudden passion. "I once entrusted the house to you... now, I do so again."

Suddenly spent and falling back onto his pillow, the German began coughing, but he raised his hand weakly as if to quell any objection from Wingood.

"I do not mean for you to *do anything* with the site," von Hallerstein finally reassured him when the coughing fit had passed. "Technically, it is still my property, but I will never visit that place again."

A spasm of memory brought an involuntary shudder to the German's face. Now he looked at Wingood piercingly.

"But you must be the *warden,* and your duties are simple. Seal the gates of the property... Ensure that nobody ever visits that place again. No one need nor should know what has happened there. Leave Marchley Howe to fade in both form and memory."

He smiled weakly at Wingood.

"Perhaps then, all *will* indeed be well Mr. Wingood.... *Vielleicht...*"

Printed in Great Britain
by Amazon